OUT
OF
HEART

IRFAN
MASTER

HOT
KEY
BOOKS

First published in Great Britain in 2017 by
HOT KEY BOOKS
80–81 Wimpole St, London W1G 9RE
www.hotkeybooks.com

A CIP catalogue record for this book is available from the British Library.

ISBN: 978-1-4714-0507-5
also available as an ebook

1

This book is typeset using Atomik ePublisher
Printed and bound by Clays Ltd, St Ives Plc

Hot Key Books is an imprint of Bonnier Zaffre Ltd,
a Bonnier Publishing company
www.bonnierpublishing.com

For MK,
who mended my wings.

The Little Boy Lost

Father, father, where are you going?
O do not walk so fast!
Speak, father, speak to your little boy,
Or else I shall be lost.

The night was dark, no father was there,
The child was wet with dew;
The mire was deep & the child did weep,
And away the vapour flew.

William Blake

*Your heart is the size
of your clenched fist.*

Thin slivers of light plunged through the square attic windows on Marrow Street. The small room in the Shah family house was a real suntrap and Adam would come here to think and draw, and to leave the shadows of the day behind. He lay down, staring up through the grimy glass at the blue rectangle of sky, and pulled out his battered, smudged notepad and a well-chewed pencil.

Suntrap. Sun trapped. Trapped son.

Adam started sketching, trying to capture the sunlight in his drawing, but soon threw his pencil down in frustration. Then an image unfolded in his brain, a painting his art teacher, Mrs Matheson, had shown him. It was of Icarus, the boy who flew too close to the sun, and showed him lying on the rocks, the ground beneath strewn with feathers. He'd soared high, letting the winds carry him, to show his father he wasn't scared. To show he could go higher. To show that he loved him. Adam understood then how you drew the sun – by showing broken wings on the rocks below. But Adam was more interested in Icarus *before* the fall. He seized his pencil and started drawing furiously. He drew Icarus, standing on the edge of the cliff looking down, wings unfurled, about to jump. Then he sketched the blurry shape of Icarus's father, Daedalus. As he traced Icarus's wings with his index finger, Adam imagined Daedalus saying, *Don't fly too close to the sun or you'll perish. Promise me you won't fly too close to the sun?* In his mind's eye, he saw Icarus turning to say, *We have nothing to fear from the sun, Father. The sun gives us life.* Adam saw Icarus spread his wings and smile, and, with a last look at his father, jump.

East London. Now.

Adam watched as the needle-thin second hand continued its sweep around the clock face. As he listened to the voice speaking on the end of the telephone, he wondered why time hadn't stopped.

Sorry, the surgeon said. *Loss*, he said. *Difficult time*, he said. His voice was quiet, almost a whisper. The right sort of voice for the wrong kind of news, Adam thought. Switching the phone to his right hand, he picked up the pencil and started sketching on the notepad next to the phone.

'What was the exact time of death?' Adam asked.

'Excuse me?'

'You always note the time of death, don't you?'

'Yes, but that's . . . It's not a question we usually get asked.'

'But can you tell me?'

'How old are you?'

'Eighteen,' Adam lied. Fifteen, eighteen, what difference did it make? Now that his grandfather, his Dadda, was dead.

'I can find out for you.'

'OK.'

Adam heard the phone being set down and the shuffling of papers. He began to add numbers to the hearts he had sketched, making them into clocks. Six hearts joined together to form one big heart.

The voice came back on the line.

'Time of death was 7.12 p.m.'

Adam drew the time onto one of the heart/clocks.

'Thank you.'

'Please can you ask your mum to call us on this number as soon as she gets home.'

Adam jotted the number down, and continued giving shape to the hearts. He looked up at the clock. 8.04 p.m. He sketched that onto another heart/clock.

Adam stared at the second hand still sweeping around the clock face and then down at the phone still in his hand. Time hadn't stopped, and all he was left with was a dead tone.

A woman's heart beats faster than a man's.

Adam stood in the doorway watching his mum. When he had told her the news, she had stood still, clenched her fists and nodded, and gone back to what she was doing. He had hoped she would look up at him, come over and hug him, hold his hand, but she hadn't. She hadn't done that in a long time.

'What you up to, Mum?'

She had her back to him and was bent over an ironing board. Next to her, piled high, was a laundry basket of crumpled clothes, waiting to be ironed. In the next room he could hear his grandmother. She was whispering to herself. A mantra. A prayer. For comfort. That was the proper response to bad news. Prayer. Words. Some tears. Right? Adam leaned against the door frame. His mum unfolded one of his shirts and laid it on the ironing board. She pressed down hard, smoothing out any creases. The board creaked. She looked up.

'Lots to be done for tomorrow,' she said.

Noticing her eyes on him, Adam looked down at his black T-shirt, black trousers and black trainers. His uniform. All black. She didn't like that and neither did his dad. They both hated that Adam wore black every day.

'Black again. Don't you have any other clothes? It's depressing.'

'I don't know why it annoys you so much. I like it, Mum.'

But his mum didn't reply. She had turned away, moving quickly, efficiently, through the laundry.

Adam knew his wearing black annoyed his mum, but at least it made her look at him. Adam sighed and took out his notepad.

Daddadead. Dad dead. Dead is dead.

Around the words he drew the shape of an ironing board and sketched an iron about to press down on the words. He looked up to see his mum standing there with her arms folded across her chest. Whereas Adam was tall, she was short, her long rust-brown skirt making her look shorter. A cream roll-neck sweater left only her face exposed. An oval face with dark eyes. Black.

'You gonna stand there scribbling or help me clean up this mess?'

Grabbing a bed-sheet, she threw one end to him. Adam found the edges and held them up. She moved forward, pinched the edges from him and squared off the sheet. Once. Twice. Perfect square. Adam knew she didn't need his help to do this, but he stood there in the hope she might say something, anything, about his Dadda. Adam had had a whole speech worked out in his bedroom, but standing here, divided by a white sheet, he couldn't find the words. She grabbed another sheet and they did the same, neither saying anything. Until all the sheets were folded, squared off and ready to be put away.

She searched for something else to iron. To fold. To put away.

'There's nothing else, Mum.'

Suddenly folding in on herself, she slumped down on the edge of the bed. Adam showed the sketch of the iron and the words he had scribbled down. She took the notepad and stared at the page. She smoothed down the curled-up edges and placed the notepad on her lap. She didn't cry. Adam wanted her to. He needed her to cry. He wanted to throw the sheets on the floor, unmake the bed, create a mess. If she didn't cry, then how could she move on, do what you need to do next? Adam sat down heavily beside her. He desperately wanted to draw the confusion that was in his head. He knew whatever he drew would be all scribbles-streaks-slashes. He knew it wouldn't make sense, but sketching it out would help him to make sense of the world around him. He just needed to draw.

He could hear the faint whisper of the prayer from his Daddima in the next room. One word over and over. *God*. Like the ticking of a clock.

Adam's little sister, Farah, was sitting with her book in the living room. A small, heart-shaped face with a fringe and a little ponytail. And her big book. Always her big book of dot-to-dots. She signed abruptly and left the room.

'What'd she say?' asked Adam's mum.

'Not sure. It was too fast. I don't think it meant anything. It was more frustration, I think.'

'She knows Dadda's gone? Did you tell her?'

'No! Mum – I thought you had.'

'I've been meaning to . . . But I don't know what to say. She's eight, she doesn't understand . . .'

Adam looked at his mum's furrowed brow. He couldn't remember the last time she had smiled.

'I'm fifteen, Mum. I don't know how to explain stuff to an eight-year-old girl.'

She looked right at him then. Sat up in her chair.

'Adam, I want you to do something. It might be hard. *Will* be hard.'

Adam didn't ask what it was. It was coming whether he liked it or not. He waited. 'I want you to be there when they wash and dress the body. I don't want it to be your dad, or for the funeral. I want you to be there. To represent us.'

Adam's mind spun. He wanted to grab his pencil, his lifeline, and write. To draw. To hear that scrape of pencil on paper. He drew a mental image of a square, a window, a horizon, a ship, birds. He always did this to calm down. But this time the image blurred.

'Adam?'

'OK, I'll go. Represent us,' he whispered.

'Good. *Good*.' Adam's mum sighed. 'Adam . . . There's something else.'

Adam heard serious in her voice. His mum was looking down at her skirt, smoothing out the pleats.

'He did something. Dadda did something without telling us. Before he died. You'll see when you go to wash the body . . .'

'See what?'

'What he did to himself. What he gave away.'

'What? What did he give away?'

'His heart, Adam. Dadda gave away his heart.'

It was still early when Adam woke. He closed his eyes again, but knew that sleep had fled. He picked up his notepad from under his pillow and made a list:

Adam Shah's to do list:
1. *Wash Dadda's body (Represent Us)*
2. *Attend Dadda's funeral*
3. *Go to school and pretend to listen*
4. *Discuss death, hearts etc. with Farah*
5. *Try to cry*
6. *Make Mum cry (or try to)*

Adam pulled the covers over his head, closed his eyes and began to draw shapes onto the dark canvas of his mind.

Early Egyptians believed that the heart and other major organs had a will of their own and would move around inside the body.

The day was dripping with sunlight. Feeling the warmth on his face and arms, Adam wished it was grimy-grey-bleak. Being asked to go and wash your grandfather's dead body was one thing, but being asked to do it when the sun was shining and everyone else was smiling and sitting in their gardens was wrong. Taking out his notepad, he scribbled.

Wrong sun. Wrong son. Wrong 'un

When his uncle arrived, Adam was looking up at the sky, his shock of roughly chopped black hair falling back from his face.

'What you looking at up there, son? He'll be up there, you know, in heaven. Watching over you,' said Idris, his voice firm. 'You can be sure of that.'

Adam wasn't sure of anything. He had never thought of his Dadda as someone who would watch over anybody. He had always been there, but never fully present, choosing silence instead of telling them what was in his head. Now

21

that he was gone, Adam had so many questions and no way of getting answers.

'Well, get in the car then, and let's get going, eh.'

It was slow driving. Adam looked out at the terraced houses packed tightly together shoulder to shoulder, each the same as the next, car out front, three steps, window downstairs, two windows up. Door. He scribbled on his notepad.

Adam's uncle glanced at him in the mirror and shook his head at the fact that Adam had chosen to sit in the back and not said a word. Instead the boy had pulled out his notepad and begun to draw.

They arrived at the hospital and parked up. Adam looked down at the maze he'd drawn, made up of square blocks. He'd lost track somewhere in the middle and now wondered if he'd left a way out. He'd give the drawing to Farah later and see if she could find a way. She was good at mazes.

He'd been visiting the hospital for the past month. Visiting his grandfather in the 'death ward' or the 'organ-failing ward'. Or the 'waiting-for-bits ward'. He'd come up with quite a few names for the place. He hated it there. Mum had always told him hate is too strong a word and that you shouldn't hate anything. Adam agreed. It *was* a strong word. That's why he used it. He *hated* it there. Hated the hospital smell. Hated the groans of suffering. Hated the waft from bland-looking food that followed him down the corridor. But most of all Adam hated the fact that there was no colour there. The hospital was colourless, as if someone had rubbed out all the colour between the lines of the walls-floors-ceilings. It was filled with nothing.

They waited in the hospital reception for two of Adam's cousins. They were running late. *It's hard to get time off work,* Idris explained. That's why they're doing this in their lunch break. They arrived in their work clothes. One was a butcher and the other an accountant. Adam privately called them Blood and Money.

'How are you, son?' asked Blood.

'Yeah. I'm fine.'

'Don't you worry too much about anything in there. It's good that you're here. Representing. You understand. Sign of a man,' said Money.

Adam wondered what sort of a sign. A scared-looking boy dressed in black with a well-thumbed notepad didn't seem like a sign of anything.

The nurse came and led them to the room. A colourless room bathed in light. In the middle was a bench on which his Dadda lay. In state, Adam thought they called it.

In state. In a state. Inner state.

His fingers were itching to scribble these words down, but his uncles looked grim so he forced himself to leave his notepad in his back pocket. The previous evening, Adam had googled 'wash body death funeral' and had received thousands of hits about ancient rituals from around the world. No matter what religion you belonged to or what you believed, there was always some kind of ritual. Some kind of death preparation. However you went about it, in order to meet God, you had to be prepared.

* * *

His cousins stepped up to the bench. Adam made to follow but his legs wouldn't obey. He was in a room with a dead body. His Dadda lay there under the sheet. Adam realised he was beside himself with terror. He bunched his jaw, his breathing ragged. Blood and Money set about the room with purpose, but Idris saw Adam frozen to the grey floor and came over.

'It's OK, son. Breathe. Otherwise you're going to pop like a balloon. Breathe, son.'

Adam looked at his uncle and let out a long gasp of air and set his shoulders.

Taking a step towards the body, Adam watched as Blood and Money washed their hands and put on rubber gloves. Pulling out a shower head, they tested it in a sink and turned to Idris, who had also put gloves on. Adam was shocked. The ancient pictures and instructions he had seen on the internet had been about bathing and cleansing using a clay pot and an earthenware jug. Items made from mud and heat and water. He had not expected rubber gloves and a shower head. It was too modern – too stainless steel-efficient-scientific. Too *cold*. He wanted to yank the sheet aside and give his Dadda a hug. To clutch at his index finger like he used to when he was tiny and learning to walk. To hear his Dadda wake early in the morning and plod slowly down the creaky stairs. The room was completely silent, but Adam could hear a rushing wind inside his head. Closing his eyes, he imagined it to be a typhoon. A swirl of air so powerful it would lift you off your feet.

'Adam, open your eyes. You must see,' said Idris in a reverent tone. They had uncovered Dadda's face and were ready to begin. The shock of seeing his Dadda lying there unnerved Adam. His Dadda's eyes were open. Adam grabbed hold of the bench and felt a chill as the metal sent a stabbing coldness up his arm. He started to tremble. Why were his eyes open?

Idris turned to Adam. 'You're a man now, so be a man. There's nothing to be scared of here. We must prepare him so he can go to God. You see his eyes are open. This is how it always is. He is watching to see who has come to send him on his way.'

Using the spray from the shower head, Idris began to wash the body, which was still mostly covered. Money stood back and uttered prayers in a quiet voice, while Blood gently turned the body so that Idris could wash parts of it. Adam watched him and realised why he was there. Blood was a butcher. He worked with dead meat every day.

Idris turned to Adam and nodded. 'Go and fill that jug over by the sink. Bring it to me,' he asked.

Returning, Adam made to hand Idris the jug.

'No, this is for you to do. Tip the water where I tell you.'

Following his instructions, his hand trembling, Adam tipped the jug and watched the water sluice over his Dadda's nut-brown skin. Blood moved across the body and pulled the sheet down to reveal Dadda's chest. Everybody froze. The tip of the scar reached down from the top of his breastbone and, like a slash, ended where the stomach began. It was pink, raised and angry-looking. It hadn't healed. Would never heal. Adam couldn't stop himself – he took out his notepad and drew the shape of the scar. His uncle and cousins turned to him.

'What are you doing?' asked Blood.

'The scar. Can you see? It's in the shape of an alif. The Arabic letter *A*. Do you see? Like *A* for Adam. He's given away his heart, but he'll be OK because the alif is where his heart used to be. For protection.' Drawing the symbol underneath, Adam scribbled a few words.

Alif. Alife. Alive. A Life

Blood tutted and covered the body once more. Idris looked strangely at Adam and continued with the ritual. Adam took a step back and stared into the bright light until his eyes hurt and began to stream with tears. But no matter where he looked, he knew his Dadda was looking only at him.

'Understanding is the heartwood of well-spoken words.'

Buddha

Farah sat on the bottom step and watched her brother. He stared back at her.

'What?'

Farah signed that he looked very serious.

'A funeral is serious, Farah. There'll be lots of serious stuff going on.'

Why can't I come? she signed.

'No women allowed.'

Why not?

'I'm not sure.'

I can be serious too. As long as I can bring my book. And my pen.

'It's not up to me, Farah. But I agree. You're one of the most serious people I know.'

I can wear black clothes too. Then everybody will definitely think I'm serious.

'I don't wear black so people think I'm seri— Look, you can't come. Sorry. I'll see you later,' Adam finished, and walked out.

Farah sat on her step and watched as the door slammed shut. Tucking in her legs, she placed the big book onto her knees, opened it and began to draw.

Your heart is not red.

Adam stood watching as the wooden coffin was lofted into the air and onto the arms of men. A queue began to form and the coffin was passed from hand to hand, shoulder to shoulder and slowly, steadily began to move forward.

'Come on, get it onto your shoulder a couple of times before it gets to the grave,' said Idris, moving past him towards the procession. He had lifted the coffin onto his shoulders and he beckoned to Adam, who moved in alongside and grabbed the handle. Hoisting it onto his shoulders, he felt the weight and almost stumbled, but pushed up and walked along. Throngs of men followed in the wake of the coffin. At fifteen, this was his first funeral. He was bearing his Dadda to the grave. Heartless.

Heartless. Hurtless. Less hurt. Less heart.

Adam suddenly realised that he hadn't brought his notepad with him. So like a mantra he began to utter the words that had come to him. Out of the corner of his eye he saw some familiar faces. Standing apart from the procession were his mum and sister. Passing the coffin onto another man's shoulder, he walked over to where they stood.

Farah signed to him. *You see, I can be serious too.*

Adam looked at her dressed all in black and smiled.

Then, 'Mum, you're not supposed to be here,' he whispered, looking behind him. Some of the men had noticed them and were pointing and signalling in their direction.

'Never mind that.' Yasmin bent down and grabbed a handful of dark brown earth. 'Here,' she said. 'Make sure you throw this into the grave.'

Adam took the damp soil and bunched it in his fist.

Hearing footsteps behind him, he saw Idris walking towards them.

'Go on. I'll see you at home,' said Yasmin.

Adam moved past Idris, holding the soil carefully in his hands.

'You shouldn't be here,' said Idris quietly.

'I have every right to be here,' replied Yasmin.

'It's not about right, it's just not appropriate—'

'What's not appropriate about a daughter and granddaughter coming to see off their Dadda?'

'Listen, daughter, you can mourn him just as well from home—'

'How well did you know him, uncle?'

'I knew him well enough. He was my cousin.'

'I knew him. You understand. Like a daughter does. How well do any of these men know him. Knew him?'

'You should go,' insisted Idris.

'No.'

Men were turning to watch them as their voices carried over the graveyard. Idris's shoulders dropped. He turned to look at the procession and walked back to join the throng. Adam watched him walk away from his mum and sister and breathed deeply, grateful that his uncle had backed off.

The body, wrapped in a shroud of simple white cotton, was removed from the coffin and lowered carefully down into the grave. As Adam watched it disappear into the hole, he felt sick. He wanted to cry. He looked over to his mum. She wasn't crying, but he hoped she would soon. She needed to cry, more than he did. The ball of mud in his hand was cold and wet. Earth created life, gave birth to flowers, fruits and food. He wanted to smear the mud across his Dadda's chest. To spread it across his scar and seal it with the earth.

The 'lub-dub' of a heartbeat is the sound made by the four valves of the heart opening and closing.

Sorry to hear, sorry to hear, so many people so sorry. Adam walked through the neighbourhood and wished he could draw himself a black hole and be sucked into it. He wanted to scream at his Dadda for leaving them behind. As his father was not living with them it was his role now to look after the family, but it weighed on him heavily, making Adam drag his feet, his head fall.

Adam walked to school slowly, taking his time, knowing he would probably be late. He also knew that he could say that his grandfather had died and so wouldn't get into trouble. When he reached the canal path he stopped to admire the graffiti under each bridge, trying to spot new tags and interesting designs. He hadn't decided on his own tag yet. He couldn't decide on a word or symbol that defined him. He'd flick through his notepad but had come up with nothing. It *had* to define him. The bell went just as Adam arrived at school. He stopped at the gate and watched everybody rushing to registration. Leaning against a wall, Adam waited for the clamour to pass.

'Are you OK?' a voice asked.

Adam looked up and saw Laila, a girl from his year, standing in front of him.

'I . . . I don't know.'

Laila stood close enough for Adam to see her light green eyes. Sometimes they were grey, but today they were green. Her hair was wild, as always, and her pale skin was touched with a little pink. She'd been running.

'You're going to be late. No use running, then being late,' said Adam.

She looked right at him with her green-grey eyes.

'I was running to catch up with you. I hope you feel less sad.' She threw her rucksack over her shoulder as she turned and walked into the school.

Adam watched her go and knew that he had said the wrong thing. However much he wanted to, he rarely said the right thing around her.

Adam always sat at the back in class, closest to the window. He did his best to listen, but as his mum often said, *Listening isn't the same as hearing.* She liked to pull that one out on him from time to time.

Adam floated through the day. He sat in maths and saw fragments of formulas jumble before his eyes. He heard dates, times, places, events in history. He stood in science for reactions and results. And in English he read and wrote words, words, words. In art, he sat in front of a blank page and waited.

Adam looked up at his art teacher, Mrs Matheson. In his mind he always thought of her as 'Kindly'. It was in her eyes. Mrs Matheson watched Adam sitting staring at the blank page. He was usually distant, but today he was in another place entirely. She flicked through his portfolio and shook her head. Adam wasn't the best sketcher in the class. Neither was his composition accurate or realistic or pretty to look at. He would probably scrape a pass in the exams. But his work was undefined. She had tried to tell him that he was able to capture something in each sketch instinctively. He had that rare ability to not filter what he was thinking and put it on the page. Not a single piece could be categorised. To be honest, his work confounded her. Made her think. Made her look again.

'It's OK, Adam, you don't have to do anything today. You can just sit.'

So Adam just sat. Art was his favourite subject, along with English. In either, he could draw and write and feel connected. He never felt more connected than when his pencil touched paper. Like a plug in a socket, he felt energy pulse up his arm and throughout his body. The art rooms had big windows. Usually light helped him think. Helped him concentrate. That's why he liked the attic room at home. But today no amount of light could help. His thoughts were jagged.

Mrs Matheson walked over and sat opposite him. She didn't speak. He'd have hated it if she'd asked if he was OK – how was he feeling, how was it at home and all that crap. Instead she sat and drew. She covered the page in vortices. Little ones, big ones, overlapping one another until the page was covered in swirls. Then she used paint, black and red and yellow, delicately adding little strands to give more shape until each vortex was spinning with angry streaks of colour. When she'd finished, she stood up, looked at him and nodded. Adam looked down at his page and at the vortices and put the pencil down. His heart was surrounded by vortices. He understood something then and, picking up his pencil, he drew the shape of a heart. Across the heart, like a slash, he drew an alif. Mrs Matheson walked past and stopped to look over his shoulder. Smiling, she nodded as the bell called for the end of the day.

The idea of the heart having two sides echoes the biblical image of the two tablets of the law, written in the heart.

William Tide stood across the road from number thirty-four Marrow Street. He stared at the grimy yellow door and wondered what he was doing there. Before he knew it, his feet were carrying him across the road. He saw his hand bunch into a fist and rap on the door. He waited, half hoping it wouldn't open. But the yellow door was pulled ajar and in front of him stood a little girl. Tipping her head to the side, she looked at him curiously.

'Hello . . . I'm . . . You don't know me . . . I just . . .' William stopped. He didn't know what to say, what he was doing here.

Farah took a step forward right up to the threshold and stared right at him. She signed at William. He looked at her in confusion, not understanding, his need to bolt threatening to overwhelm him. He suddenly realised how he must look to her in his ill-fitting charity clothes – his too-small wax jacket, his too-short trousers and his too-pale face. She signed at him again.

'I don't understand.'

Behind the girl, floating down, there was a voice.

'Who is it, Farah?'

'I should go,' said William, poised to flee.

Farah held out her hand in a gesture that made him pause. Behind her, a young woman emerged and came to stand behind Farah, her hand gathering the door ready to shut it in his face.

'No, thank you, we don't need anything,' she said.

'I haven't got anything to sell,' said William.

'Then what are you doing here?'

Farah turned to her mum and signed again.

Yasmin shook her head. 'I doubt it very much, Farah.'

William saw the exchange between mother and daughter and heard footsteps behind them. A boy, dressed all in black, stood watching, dark eyes sizing up William.

'What did she sign?' asked William.

'She said she recognised you,' replied Adam, surprised and curious. He looked at Farah and then at William, wrestling with something in his head. 'No, that's not right,' continued Adam. 'It's difficult to explain, but she didn't say that she recognised you as such, but something about you.'

'Who are you? And what do you want?' Yasmin asked in a firm voice, dark eyes flashing.

William looked at all three faces, and then down at the three steps leading to their door.

'I should go,' he said, losing his nerve.

'No, wait! Why did you come?' asked the boy.

'I . . . I'm not exactly sure . . . It's hard to explain. My name's William Tide. I have a heart in my chest that belongs to you. To your family. To Mr Abdul-Aziz Shah.'

Turning, Farah signed to her mum and Adam. *You two never listen to me. I told you I recognised him.*

The three members of the Shah family stood and stared at the man with their grandfather's heart. Adam stepped past his mother and pulled the door open.

'Do you want to come in?' he asked.

William went up the three steps and over the threshold into the Shah family house.

Farah was the first to turn and beckon him inside. He followed her into the living room.

'What are you doing?' said Yasmin in a furious whisper to Adam.

Adam closed the front door and walked past her into the kitchen. Yasmin followed him in and shut the door. Daddima, Adam's grandmother, was busy chopping onions, preparing a meal.

Pointing at the door, Yasmin shook her head.

'You just let some random guy into our house. Because he said some nonsense about whatever.'

'Why would it be nonsense? Did you see Farah? She sensed something about him.'

'Even if it's true, what are we supposed to do about it? With it? I mean, he's not . . . I don't know.'

'I don't know either. It . . . just made sense.'

'No. It makes no sense. None of this makes no sense. So Dadda dies. Doesn't say a word to us about his heart-donation crap. Doesn't tell us what he's thinking, and now two weeks later we have a strange guy in our house. Is that how it's supposed to be?'

Silence. Nothing but the dull thud of the knife on the chopping board. The cacophony in Adam's head was building. The knife, the clock ticking on the kitchen wall and, loudest of all, the steady drum of the heart in the other room.

William stood in the front room. He could hear raised voices and knew they would be about him. He'd only thought about coming and knocking on the door. Beyond that, he hadn't planned anything. He watched as the little girl moved towards the far end of the room and sat down at a small table. The light was best there. Opening her book, she began, in short sharp motions, to draw a shape. William sat down heavily in an old moss-green armchair. As he sat down, his legs gave way, like he'd been dropped into the sea with an anchor attached to his ankles. Leaning forward, he rocked back and forth slowly. Everything he now did was set to a rhythm. The rhythm of his heart. The beat of his heart. The lub-dub, his doctor called it. *Lub-dub, lub-dub.* Before his operation he'd never even thought about it, but now it was playing in his ears, like a song or a tune you just couldn't shake out of your head. He could feel it pulsing in his ears, in his chest, in the veins of his neck and in the raised threads of his wrists . . . The arms of the chair were worn and pitted in places. William let his fingers trace the grooves of the coarse material. This was Abdul-Aziz Shah's chair. Where *he* must have sat. The little girl looked over her shoulder and smiled at him. She waved. He waved back, but didn't smile. She signed something. He shrugged and pointed to himself, shaking his head, and mouthed, 'I don't understand.'

'She's asking if you feel OK,' said Adam quietly.

William turned to look at the boy standing in the doorway. He was tall and skinny as a toothpick. His face was all angles and sharp cheekbones and deep-set eyes. Eyes that were glowering at him.

'I feel different to before – odd,' replied William.

Adam glanced over to Farah, who signed a flurry of signals and went back to her book.

William looked at Adam puzzled.

'She said to tell you not to worry about it – we're all a bit odd in this family.'

William glanced over to the little girl sitting in the light and back over to the boy standing in the shadows, fingers twitching and dark eyes seeing things he could not comprehend. Putting his hand over his heart instinctively, William looked up at the boy.

'I didn't know what else to do. It's his heart. I don't know why he left it behind. I don't know why I have it. I don't know anything about him.'

Adam looked down at the big man in front of him, folded into his Dadda's armchair.

'You're not the only one,' he replied, and walked out of the room.

'Surely there is in the body a small piece of flesh; if it is good, the whole body is good, and if it is corrupted, the whole body is corrupted, and that is surely the heart.'

Prophet Muhammad (PBUH)

Adam sat at the kitchen table sipping a cool glass of milk. It had been the longest day he could remember, and still it wasn't over. The doorbell rang. He expected it to be his mum coming home from the shops.

'Yo! Wa gwan?' It was Cans, his best friend, music zinging from the headphones around his neck.

'Nuttin much. What you saying?'

'Nuttin. Thought I'd go old school and knock on your door stead of texin,' replied Cans, smiling.

And, just like that, Adam felt better. Cans bobbed to some beat in his head as he spoke. The huge headphones looked like two giant bear paws wrapped around him. The music was loud, the headphones trembling from the bass. Adam looked at his friend and grinned. Fresh trim, fresh trainers. Cans had a way of cutting through the sludge of the day with his vibesy energy.

'Come in. Want some milk?'

'Are you mad, fam? Man thinks I'm five years old or

summat. I will have some of that strong-ass Indian tea you know. That's a meal in a mug right there.'

'Awright, awright, I'll put some on. Come in then.'

Cans threw down his rucksack and followed Adam inside. As he walked past the front room, he saw William sitting there and automatically held up his hand in greeting. William waved back. Sitting down at the small table in the kitchen, Cans thumbed over his shoulder.

'Bruv, I don't want to alarm you and that, but there's some random dude sitting in your living room.'

'Yeah. That's William. He's a new addition.'

'Wha? Did you win him on eBay? Who the hell is he?'

Adam sighed. As he watched the tea brew, he explained how William had come to be there.

'That's deep, man. I mean, that's next level, voodoo heart transplantation, mind-bending deep. Deeeeeep. You get me?'

'Man turns up at your door, what can you do? You can't just turn him away – he's got a piece of your grandfather in him. What you gotta do, bruv?'

'Can't tell you. Too deep for me, fam. I'm a simple guy. I like simple tings. Music, girls and barbecue chicken. In that order.'

Adam smiled. Cans was one of the brightest people he knew.

'Speaking of girls, what's that one you like sayin? Green eyes, what's her name?'

'Laila. I didn't see her today. She's OK.'

'OK? Is that it? I see you two standing close, all deep connection and that. What's going on? I know she likes you.'

'I don't know, man. I always say the wrong thing around her. She says something nice, I say something stupid. She's understanding and patient, I do something that makes me look a wasteman.'

'You do have that mysterious-outsider thing down pat.'

'What mysterious-outsider thing?'

'Never mind. Look, in my opinion, there's never a situation where music isn't the answer. I have the solution to your social awkwardness.'

'Yeah, a rope, a bridge and a gentle push . . .'

'If that's all you got, try not speaking! I think a few pointers from Farah might help – stick to sign language. Now look, make her a mixtape of your choice tunes, you get me? Then you'll have something to talk about. You could even pick songs with coded messages in them so she gets the hint.'

'I'm no good at making playlists. I just put it on shuffle.'

'See, that's where you going wrong. It's gotta be from the heart. I can help with that. I'm gonna make you a playlist. Pick what you like and give it to her. She'll love it.'

'Awright, cool. I'll try it.'

'Cool. Awright, gotta go. Got some remixing to do.'

'Awright, man. Thanks for going old school and comin round.'

'S'cool. I would say keep it real, but it's as real as it can get with heart dude in the house.'

'A bit too real.'

'Bell me if you want it to be less real sometimes, bruv?'

Adam nodded and smiled. Cans shrugged on his rucksack, picked some music and, placing his headphones, sauntered down the street. Adam watched as he turned and, pointing to his phone, yelled, 'See? Hand-picked playlist. It's gotta come from the heart!'

Your heart is in the middle of your chest,
in between your right and left lung.
It is tilted slightly to the left.

Farah put her green pen down and turned to watch William. He was so pale he shone like a ghost sitting there in the dark room. Farah signed, *Do you want something to drink?* William shook his head. During his time in hospital, William had lost his appetite. Now, he couldn't eat anything without an acrid, metallic taste in his mouth. Yasmin entered the room, having returned from the shops, and looked at William and Farah.

'Chai,' she said, placing a mug in front of William and leaving again. William looked at the steaming mug and made to take a sip. Still watching him, Farah waved her hands and signalled for him to stop. She shook her head. *Do you want to burn your tongue?* William set the mug down. Leaning over the mug, Farah gently blew on the tea to cool it. As he sat back to watch her, William took his right hand and hooked it over his left shoulder. Something he had started to do soon after the operation, closing off his heart to the world and protecting it within.

'Is that why you don't speak? Because you burnt your tongue?' asked William.

Farah shook her head and stuck out her tongue. *My tongue's not burnt. See? I just don't like to speak.*

'She said that she doesn't like to speak,' said Adam, who had come in behind his mother. He could see that Farah was comfortable with William and had accepted his being there. It made Adam look at William in a different light.

William nodded. He thought he understood. Farah *chose* not to speak.

'There's not always a lot worth saying,' he replied.

Pleased with that answer, Farah lifted the mug and handed it to William, urging him to drink. William swallowed the sweet, milky tea and sighed. The taste reminded him of something, but the fragment of memory floated out of his reach. Taking another sip, he realised he liked the taste very much. Happy now, Farah went back to the window and her book. William watched as Farah's hand jerked from point to point, eyes scanning the page. Adam knelt down beside her.

'It's a dot-to-dot book,' he explained. 'Farah always has to have her big book of dot-to-dot. When she was just learning how to hold a pencil, she would watch me draw in my notepad and try to copy me. Since she . . . stopped talking, she can't make the connections to draw by herself or copy, but she can do dot-to-dot. She's very peaceful when she's drawing in her book.'

'Must be satisfying, using the dots to complete a finished picture.'

'Yes . . . maybe. It helps her make sense of the world.'

'And you? You like drawing – does it help you make sense of the world too?

'Sometimes it's the only thing that does help.'

Adam came to sit on the sofa, between the two, and pulled out his notebook. William watched him sketch and sank into the chair, letting the iron anchor pull him down into the dark.

He woke as he did every time since he'd left hospital, with a jolt. The doctor had told him, not long after he'd come back from surgery, that when the heart was placed into his chest it had been unresponsive and that the final procedure had been to jolt the heart alive with a shock of electricity. William kept feeling the jolt. The room was dark and Farah and Adam were no longer there. Sitting up in the chair, he rubbed his eyes.

'Daddima thinks you're Adam's tutor,' said Yasmin.

William tried to make out the dark shape sitting on the sofa opposite him. Yasmin sat, staring at William, arms folded across her chest.

'I didn't have the heart to tell her the truth,' she continued.

Still half asleep and adjusting to the dark, William looked at Yasmin and didn't say anything.

'It was meant to be a little joke. Ain't got much of a sense of humour, have ya?'

'I'm sorry – I should go,' said William, and stood up.

'Will we see you again, William?' asked Yasmin as she ushered him out.

William took in the house and the short, intense woman in front of him. He felt the anchor dragging him back down again. He touched the russet brickwork of the house wall and felt better.

'I can come back tomorrow?' said William.

Yasmin nodded.

'Good. Farah likes you. We'll see you tomorrow,' she said, and closed the door.

Hooking his right hand over his left shoulder, William walked up the street feeling like he could really do with another cup of chai.

Almost 100,000 times each day, the heart continues its steady beat.

Adam walked through the school gates, hoping he'd bump into Laila. He hadn't seen her for a few days. He hoped he'd say the right thing this time.

'Oi! Art boy! Wait up!' shouted a voice behind him.

A tall boy jogged towards him, followed by a bunch of other boys shoving each other. Adam carried on scanning the playground for Laila. The tall boy reached him first and cuffed him gently on his head.

'What's up, Art boy?'

'Nuttin. What's up with you?'

'Oh, you know, this and that, bruv.'

Adam looked at the boy standing in front of him. He and Faizal had grown up on the same street together, spending a lot of time at each other's houses as kids, but that had all stopped when Adam's mum and dad had separated. Faizal had always treated Adam like his younger brother. Although he had always been Faizal to Adam, everybody else called him Faze. But Adam didn't want to talk now. He wanted to find

Laila. Faze's friends bundled into him and sent him careering into Adam, shoving him to the ground. Adam landed hard. He got up slowly. That was the first time in a while somebody had come so close to him, let alone touched him, and it had hurt. Faze turned to the other boys and swore at them and they backed off. They wouldn't go up against Faze.

'You all right?' he asked quietly.

Adam nodded. He didn't want to speak. Didn't trust himself.

'How's your mum? And Farah?'

Nodding again, Adam looked at the floor.

'I'll come round and we can play a bit of Xbox.'

Adam nodded again. Faze hadn't been around for a few years.

'Still drawing those mad things and writing those mad words . . . ?'

'Still,' Adam replied.

'Mad kid,' replied Faze, shaking his head. 'I've got to go. See you later, bruv.'

Adam scanned the crowd as he watched Faze move away.

'What you looking for?' said a voice behind him.

He turned to see Laila looking like she'd been running again. He decided to keep his mouth shut about it this time.

'Nuttin. Jus lookin.'

'You looked far, far away.'

'Sometimes I feel far away too.'

'I get you. I feel like I'm watching myself sometimes. Are you still feeling sad about things?'

Adam shook his head and looked at his feet. Lifting up her hand, she almost brushed his chin and like magic made him look up again.

'I don't mean to upset you,' she said quietly.

Adam looked at her wavy, wild black hair and saw the world reflected in her green-grey eyes. Wanted to draw it.

'You're a funny, quiet boy,' she said.

'I know I'm weird.'

'No, I meant it in a different way, a good—' she said.

'I know I'm different. And weird. Weirdly different.'

'No. No, you're not, that's not what—'

'I get it,' Adam replied.

'You don't get it. You don't understand anything,' she huffed, and walked past him. He watched her go, wild hair trailing behind her, and took out his notepad.

Looking hard. Lookhard. Hardlook. Hard luck.

When Adam got home from school the last thing he had expected was to see William sitting in his Dadda's armchair. Farah had taken up her usual position near the window. Putting down his rucksack, Adam walked into the kitchen. His mum was still at work and Daddima was probably having a nap upstairs. Walking back into the living room, Adam went to stand by Farah.

'Have you had something to eat?'

Farah looked up and nodded. *I had some tea with William. He doesn't really say much.*

'Neither do you,' Adam replied.

Thinking about it for a second, she signed, *True*, and went back to her book.

Adam looked at William.

'Why'd you come back?'

'Your mum asked if I would and . . . I said yes. It felt right,' he replied quietly. 'Do . . . ? Do you mind?'

Adam hesitated, then shook his head. He moved to a drawer and pulled out a photograph of his grandfather, Abdul-Aziz

Shah. It showed him on his wedding day, surrounded by family and friends.

'Is that him?' William asked.

'Yeah.'

'He looks happy,' said William, taking the photograph from Adam.

'He might have been then. I don't know – he was always kind to us, but he never really properly talked to us.'

'But he had you and Farah, his wife and your mum. He had all of that.'

'He never let us know what he was thinking. Not even the heart thing. He lived inside his head.'

Adam looked over at William. In the shadows lingering in the living room, William could have been his Dadda sitting in the moss-green armchair.

'Why did you come here, William?' asked Adam.

'I had no choice. I left the hospital and just started walking . . .'

'We've been through a lot. We're trying to forget things and move on. You're reminding us of things we need to forget,' said Adam suddenly, feeling like he wanted to cry. Just looking at William stirred something in him.

'Your Dadda? Why would you want to forget him?'

'Because he lived in his own world! And he forgot about us! Leaving his heart behind, that's just cruel. Sending you to us. That's just one big joke!' Adam found he was shouting.

'You think he sent me to you? I'd never thought of it like that,' whispered William.

'What do you WANT FROM US?' demanded Adam, stopping pacing and standing in the middle of the room.

'I don't want anything . . . I don't know, Adam, I'm sorry. I know I've just ended up here, with your family, but . . .'

Adam picked up his rucksack and stomped up the stairs.

Snapping the lid back onto her green felt-tip pen, Farah went to stand by William.

He's not angry at you.

William shrugged his shoulders, not really understanding what Farah was trying to say.

He's just serious all the time. He thinks he has to look after us now.

'He thinks he has to be the man of the house now?'

Looking at him strangely, she signed, *That's what I meant.*

She hopped off the armchair and went back to her book. Turning, she smiled. *Ask him about his drawings. He's got books full of drawing and words. Ask him. You'll see, he'll talk. He won't be angry.*

William watched her fluttering hands and tried to concentrate. What was she trying to say? He tried to piece it together. Farah had smiled throughout. Whatever it was she had signed, it was positive. He'd caught a few of her signs – *talk, words, drawings, book* . . . William sank back into the chair and rubbed his eyes.

Adam pulled his hoody over his head and waited. The disused railway yard was deserted. He looked over at the old trains packed tightly together – a place where trains came to die. Adam thought about his grandfather, about donating your self so that another person could live. Everywhere people were recycling things, saving them so they could be used again. Rebuilt and reconstructed.

Reuse. Refuse. Refuel. Refuge.

Staring at the words he had scribbled in his notebook, Adam shook his head. He knew scribbling random words down in the middle of conversations was odd, but he didn't know how else to hold on to his thoughts. No wonder Laila looked at him in that way. He put his pad away and waited. He knew they'd be here. This was where they always came, every day, for a smoke and to try out their new cans. He wasn't part of their crew, not really, and the only reason they tolerated him was because he could really spray and he was discreet. Adam knew about all their tagging spots, but he knew to keep quiet. Two boys with rucksacks approached him.

'Awright, bruv, you cool? Thought it was one of those Bow youts. They been taking piss recently. Stealin our best spots. Long ting,' said the short stocky boy known as Tank.

'I saw them earlier, near that industrial park down the road from the warehouses,' replied Adam.

'That used to be a top spot for us. Been rinsed now,' he replied, shaking his head.

The other boy still hadn't spoken. He was much taller than Adam and had a little strip of beard. His name was Paul, but he liked to be known as Strides. Adam knew that Strides didn't really think Adam should be there. Adam didn't have a tag and he didn't really hang with the crew. He was an interloper. In any crew, you had to be there. You had to belong. Adam didn't. They both set their rucksacks down and lit up.

'Wanna drag?'

'Nah. I'm good,' replied Adam.

71

Strides took a deep pull on his cigarette and spat.

'You don't have a tag, you don't really crew with us and you don't want to smoke with us. What good is you to us, bruv?'

'Nah, come on, leave it, Strides, he's all right. He's cool. Man can spray, right.'

Adam went to his rucksack. 'I'll go if you want. Don't want no problems.'

'Nah, come on, you're all right. Stay, do a bit of work. Tag something, cuz,' said Tank.

Strides didn't say anything, and Adam put down his rucksack, grabbed a few cans and started to walk away.

'Where you going?'

'To tag something,'

'But the wall's here, bruv. What you going to tag? The trains? They all been mostly done. This here wall still has some canvas,' said Tank, pointing with his can to the large breeze-block wall.

'I have an idea for something. Something that might take some time.'

'Oh yeah. What's that?'

'Can't explain. You'll have to see as I do it,' Adam replied throwing his hood over his head and lifting up the black scarf around his neck to cover his face, leaving only his eyes exposed.

Both boys looked on as Adam, merging with the shadows, walked towards the trains. Climbing up onto the nearest one, Adam looked over the tops of the closely packed carriages. Huddled together, discarded, set apart. *Dead machinery*. Adam quickly sketched the plan that had been forming in his head onto his notepad, taking note of the formation of the trains. It was perfect. They were almost symmetrical. A large square expanse of metal. A clear canvas. He looked up, eyes tracing the surrounding estate blocks, noting the lights flickering in each flat. *Watch me now.* Tying a scarf around his mouth, he shook the spray can and heard the metal ball bearing rattle. He pressed down on the nozzle, and the paint sprayed down onto the grey metal. Adam was satisfied with the colour – a splash of blood red. He took off his hoody and set to work.

William had been lying in his hospital bed for almost two weeks when Dr Desai had come over with a big smile on his face. Opposite him, there was an empty bed with newly laid crisp white sheets. 'William, are you ready for this? We're going to get you living. We have a heart for you,' he'd said. William remembered being surprised. He'd signed up for it. He'd gone through the tests. Had prepared himself that it could happen. Realised that the right thing to do would be to fight. To stay alive. He'd never for one second thought it could actually happen. Now that the moment was here, William felt a kind of disappointment. He was going to live – when for so long he'd expected to die. He hadn't been able to say anything at the time, and the doctor had mistaken that for shock and congratulated him. As the nurses fussed about William and pushed him in his bed out of the death ward, he spotted a set of prayer beads on the floor. He made the nurses stop to scoop them up and entwined them around his hand.

Breathing in the scent of sandalwood, he sank further into the bed. William knew only one thing with certainty. That for the doctor to give him that news, someone had died . . .

'Most people were heartless about turtles because a turtle's heart will beat for hours after it has been cut up and butchered. But the old man thought, I have such a heart too.'

Ernest Hemingway, The Old Man and the Sea

Sitting in the canteen eating his lunch, Adam looked out of the big windows and saw clumps of kids walking, talking, laughing and jostling. The noise was incredible. It created static in his head. A constant burring sound that made him close his eyes and put his hands over his ears.

'Adam, you awright?' Cans's busy vibe penetrated the static.

Adam shook his head to clear his thoughts and opened his eyes.

'I'm just tired. Didn't sleep too good.'

'Me neither. I was listening to some tunes, bruv, you wouldn't believe. Some mixtapes that were crazy. Serious bruv, craaazy.'

'But you're going to remix them right. Splice and dice?'

'You know me, fam. It could be good, but Cans can make it better for sure.'

Adam looked at Cans and the light that came to his eyes when he talked about music, the way he became animated when he was talking about a new track he'd discovered. Adam imagined Cans's brain to work like a turntable. Record turning.

Taking out his pad, he sketched a few things down. Cans looked up from his pudding and shook his head.

'Bruv, you know that I get your whole silent drawing, faraway deep thing. But whipping out your sketchpad and pencil, guy, remember, we spoke about this? Girls think that stuff is weird. Boys will murder you for it. And teachers gonna think you need some kind of counselling. That you is on some autistic spectrum. They gonna put you in some room with a *psycho*-analyst sayin, "And what do you see when you look at this?" And when you say *butterflies*, they write dead cows or summat. You'll be admitted, bruv.'

Adam smiled, but carried on sketching while Cans scraped out the last of his pudding. Finishing the sketch, Adam flipped the pad shut.

'And?' said Cans.

'And what?'

'What did you draw, bruv? You got all busy with the HB nib, and then what? You ain't gonna show me?'

'You said it was weird. Said I was a mental case.'

'Nah, I didn't say that. I said *others* would say it . . . Oi, stop distractin me and let me have a look, fam.'

Adam flipped open his pad and slid it over to Cans.

A big grin appeared on his face as he held up the pad. 'This is mad. Can I keep it?'

'You like it?'

'Bruv, I love it. I can use this on my next promo when I'm DJing. If that's OK with you? Don't want no legal wrangling when I make it though.' He chuckled.

'You can have it and use it. Course, bruv.'

Cans looked at the drawing of a skull. In the frontal lobe, Adam had sketched Cans on a turntable listening to the playback. At the bottom, graffiti-style, he had written '*Loony Tunes*' – Cans's DJ name.

'Tear it off for me. I don't want to ruin it,' said Cans, handing the pad back to Adam. Adam carefully tore out the sheet and handed it to Cans, who tucked it into the middle of an exercise book and patted it.

Out the corner of his eye, Adam saw Laila walking towards him, but she went straight past, eyes fixed ahead.

'Jeeeeez, cuz. What you say to her?' asked Cans. 'You gave her rage.'

'The wrong thing. Always the wrong thing,' replied Adam. 'I told you.'

'Do you like her like that, bruv?'

During a typical school day, Adam would do his best to avoid mostly everyone. Everyone except Cans. Like Adam, Cans lived in his head, with his tunes. Like him, he created in his head. If he could talk to anybody, he could talk to Cans. He took a deep breath. 'I don't know what I like her like.'

'Does your heart start hitting some deep bass when she's around you?'

Adam thought about that, and hadn't really listened to or noticed his heart when he was around her.

'Nah, I don't think it's like that.'

'No?'

'Hard to explain.'

Shaking his head, Adam stood up abruptly. 'I'd better go.'

'Where? There's time still,' replied Cans.

81

'I just wanna clear my head. I'll see you later, bruv.'

Walking out of the canteen, Adam swore under his breath. Cans didn't mean anything by it. He'd asked the right questions. But Adam hated the right questions.

Since Dadda had died, Adam's mother had been working two jobs. That morning, before he'd left, Adam had seen a pile of bills on the kitchen table, marked with flashes of red. His mum was falling behind. Adam knew he had to pass his exams, but in order to help his family he would also have to get a job. Adam thought of William suddenly, and tried to shake his head clear of the strange big man. But he couldn't. He wondered if William would be sitting in the moss-green armchair when he got home.

'Hello, son.'

Adam heard the low voice right behind him, but in his head it felt like it had carried from across the oceans. He even imagined hearing it when he was born, a whispered prayer in his ear. But that was in his imagination. From things he'd been told. Happy memories he'd exchanged for bad memories. The voice was a bad memory.

'Son, hold on. Don't walk so fast, eh. Let your old man catch up.'

Adam turned to see his dad hurry to come alongside him. He was tall, still slightly taller than Adam, but there wasn't much in it. Adam could almost look him in the eye. His patchy beard was sprinkled with salt-and-pepper stubs of hair, but his hair was still jet black, a shock of unkempt hair twin to Adam's. Like Adam's, his face was all angles and cheekbones and deep-set eyes. Adam turned away suddenly, realising that looking at his dad was like looking into a mirror twenty years on. He didn't like what he saw.

'I saw you at the funeral. Saw your mum too. I knew it would be a hard day, so didn't want to cause a fuss.'

Adam nodded but looked past his dad. At the breaking sky behind him.

'How are you? How's my little girl?'

'We're all fine.'

'Yeah, good to hear, good to hear.'

Adam concentrated on the patch of sky that was still clear. Still unaffected by the grey threatening to overwhelm it. He wanted to dive right into it, before the heavens closed.

'So, no hug for the old man? No *How's it going, Dad?* How's school? You've got exams and stuff coming up, haven't you?'

Tearing his eyes from the patch of white, he looked at his dad.

'What do you want, Dad?'

Sighing, Adam's dad shrugged.

'I'm your dad. I want to see if you're OK.'

'You've seen me. I'm OK. Now what?'

They'd stopped in the middle of the street, not far from the local primary school. Groups of children floated past and around them like shoals of fish flitting around their feet. Adam and his dad were rocks entrenched in the seabed.

'I want to see you more,' he replied.

'You know Mum won't like that. She won't let that happen.'

'But you could let it happen. I know what she thinks of me, but I'm your dad. I want us to know each other.'

Adam looked into the onyx eyes of his dad, so hard to read. What was he thinking? He scanned his face for signs of fury, for the anger that was always close. Adam looked down at his dad's hands, his fists. Those fists that had caused so much damage. To his mum. To him and Farah. Fists that could break bones, fists that could break promises, fists that could break hearts.

'What's different now, Dad? What's changed from before?'

'I've changed. I'm not as . . . angry as I was. I can control it now. I know what to do. I won't hurt you again. Any of you.'

Adam pinned his eyes to the patch of sky, now steadily disappearing.

'Come on, trust me, I'm your dad. I've changed.'

Adam needed to clear his head after the meeting with his dad. He made a detour to the disused railway yard. It was empty and for a while as he set about doing his work he was lost in the mist of red paint. He thought suddenly of Laila. He knew a lot of boys said the wrong thing for appearance's sake, because it made sense to keep it cool. Adam didn't care about any of that. He cared that he came across as difficult, when all he wanted was to spend a bit of time with her. Standing back from the newly sprayed train top, Adam knew that he'd like to show her what he was doing here. Next time he saw her, he'd ask her if she would come with him, say he had a surprise for her. Putting the lids back on the cans, he gathered up his rucksack and climbed down. It was already late and a feeling of guilt washed over him. He should be home with his family, not indulging in some graffiti in this dark disused corner. His mum looked tired, her two jobs taking their toll, dark circles around her eyes. She couldn't go on like that. Adam knew how he could help.

Blood looked Adam up and down and grimaced. Wiping his hands on his apron, he threw a rack of lamb onto the worktop and began to cut it into even quarters with short sharp chopping actions.

'I need someone who clears up and gets rid of all the mess properly. Makes sure everything is nice and clean around here.'

Nodding, Adam looked at Blood. His bushy beard was straggly and had flecks of blood in it, making him look like an old warrior on a battlefield. With the cleaver in his hand, he really looked the part.

'Adam?'

'Uh, yeah?'

'I need someone that's going to listen . . . ?

'I can listen, Uncle. I can keep this place clean.'

Shaking his head and throwing a large steak onto the wooden top, Blood patted the meat flat and brought the cleaver down.

'We close every day at six thirty. Come at six to help clear up, but the main day is Saturday. I'll need you to keep the space clean and do some deliveries.'

'I can do all that, Uncle.'

'I'll give you fifty quid a week to do all that. Fair?

Adam calculated and nodded. 'Fair. Thank you.' Blood wiped his hands on his apron and produced his right hand. Adam looked at the blood-smeared hand and shook it.

'I'll see you Monday.'

'Monday,' agreed Adam.

Walking out of the shop, Adam looked at the blood already drying on his hand.

Adam turned the key in the front door and walked into the dimly lit hallway. He threw his rucksack at the foot of the stairs, kicked off his shoes and entered the front room. Empty. No Farah with her book. And no William. But there was no reason for him to be here. Adam walked into the kitchen and took a swig of milk straight from the bottle. He felt a sudden, stabbing disappointment that William wasn't sitting in the armchair. Hearing the front door open, Adam turned to see Farah walk into the kitchen. She put a bag of shopping on the kitchen table, onions spilling onto the floor. Following closely behind was Yasmin with a clutch of bags she dumped heavily, trying to avoid the onions rolling around her feet.

'And where were you today?' Yasmin asked, raising her eyebrows at Adam. 'You forgot what day it was?'

'It's supermarket Tuesday! Sorry, I forgot.'

'Yeah, I noticed. And we had nothing in the house, not even beans.'

'Sorry, Mum, I just forgot.'

'I get that, but I couldn't do it all by myself so I had my two helpers.'

'Farah's a good helper. Where's Daddima?'

'Daddima can't carry anything, you daft thing. Her fingers hurt. No, my other helper, William.'

At that moment William walked through the front door.

'He's here again,' Adam whispered.

Yasmin looked at Adam and nodded. 'Yeah, he doesn't talk much, so with him and Farah for company you have to keep yourself entertained, but it was useful to have another set of hands,' she said, with a smile.

William carefully put his shopping bags on the kitchen table and glanced at Adam.

'Here, sit,' Adam said to William, pulling out a chair.

William sat heavily. Farah signed excitedly to Adam, the only bit of which William understood was, *This is fun*.

She skipped around the kitchen picking onions up as Yasmin hummed an old song under her breath while she did the washing-up.

'Right, that's the dishes done. Who wants a cup of chai?' asked Yasmin.

Three voices said 'yes' in unison. William looked at Adam and smiled. Adam returned the smile as Farah came and sat on his lap.

'Typical. You lot should be making me tea after the day I've had . . .' Yasmin replied, but she continued humming as she turned to fill the saucepan with water.

A little later, drinking their tea, Adam studied William. He was so pale you could see the lurid green veins in his neck and face. His hair, thinning on top, rust flecked, was cropped short. He always sat in his chair like he was bracing himself for impact. Like he was about to crash.

William pointed to the notepad next to Adam.

'Is that where you dump it all? The stuff in your head.'

'Sometimes.'

'Can I see?'

'They're just scribblings and words. Random.'

'Farah told me you could really draw.'

'Did she?' replied Adam, looking over at the small figure near the window.

He passed the notebook to William.

William flicked slowly through the pages. 'These are really good.'

'They're just sketches. Nothing major,' replied Adam.

'What are you doing with these sequences of words?'

'Hard to explain.'

'Try.'

Adam looked at William.

'The words help me make sense of things. Of things I see and hear and feel. Once I write them down, things begin to make more sense in my head.'

'I understand,' replied William.

'I sound like special needs,' said Adam, shaking his head.

'We all have our own special needs,' said William gently, spotting handwriting that clearly wasn't Adam's, and written with a blue pen. Adam only ever used pencil.

'That's him, my Dadda. I found it not long after he'd gone.'

William read, and as he did so, he felt his chest tightening.

'Shame. He feels shame about something . . . within himself.'

Adam took the notebook from William and sat down.

'He was working at Russell Square station in 2005. His shift had just started when the bombs went off. The explosion shook the whole station and he helped pull people out. He never talked about it, but after, he'd sit in front of the TV, and every mention of any terrorist act, he'd hold himself rigid right there in that armchair. He hated what it made our community and people look like.

'It's the only thing I have written by him. He wrote it on the front page like he wanted me to find it. I haven't shown it to anyone else, not even Mum. I didn't know what to do with it.'

'He wanted to leave something behind. Something that wasn't hate.'

Adam stared at the words, tracing the spidery handwriting across the page. As he listened to William, something shifted in him and he felt relief. It was all he had, but it was something.

Not in my shame not in my naming and shaming
those that are not ours knots bound and found in
our homes but knotted hearts not our hearts not
this exploding bodies not us this knots of hate
not us in the 99 names shame on us for you all
our above love above your state of hate for all you
cannot for all we have for all our hearts beat fists
on doors not opened this heart left behind no
heart left behind full of above all love love above
all full of above all love love above all love above
all love above all

Adam stared at the blinking cursor, fingers hovering over the keyboard. His mind was a scramble. He never went online to chat, but something had made him log in and there she was, online, Laila. Touching the keys with the tips of his fingers, Adam pretended to type what he really felt. *I like you Laila. Do you like me?* Scowling, he lifted his fingers and slapped his forehead in disgust. *Like?* The cursor continued to blink accusingly at him. Adam stared at the message from Laila.

Adam u OK? Haven't seen you in a while . . .

Adam stood up and paced the room. Don't be an idiot – message back.

I'm cool. Been a bit busy . . .

Nothing. Adam stared at the cursor and willed it to flash some words across the screen.

She's probably gone, he took so long to get back to her.

Busy? You always rush off after school. I don't even see you in the art room any more . . . Everything OK?

Yeah it's cool. I've got a job . . .

Where?!

At the butcher's. On the High Road.

That's where we buy our meat!

Yeah

But you can't be there all the time. I NEVER see you around . . .

Dunno. Don't seem to have much time nowadays.

OK Mr NO-TIME. How about you make some time?

For what?

Adam, I sometimes wonder about what's going on in that pretty head of yours LOL

???

Make some time for me SMH

Fingers resting on the keyboard, Adam stared at the screen.

Shutting his eyes tight, he typed.

How about tomorrow . . . ?

Blink. Pause. Blink. Pause. Blink . . .

Tomorrow is perfect. At the park near school? There's a bench near the swings

I know it

After school then

Yeah

Slapping his head, Adam swore again. *Yeah?* He tried again.

That sounds good.

Great

??

That sounds great. Better than good LOL

Great
See yer tomorrow
Adam
Laila
x

Sitting back in his chair, Adam stared at the x that marked his screen. He wondered how such a small symbol could make you feel so good.

Adam Shah's To Do List:
1. Meet Laila (Be cool)
2. Meet Dad (Watch him)
3. William (Try to understand why he's here)
4. Carry on working on the >big project<.
5. Watch Mum (still needs to cry)
6. Keep it real (Cans)

Adam sat on the park bench and watched the path, waiting for Laila. The lilies nearby shivered in the wind and Adam wondered if he should pick a few for her. Would she like that or think it was corny? He stood up, started towards the flowers than paced back and sat down again. Scowling, he took out his notepad and drew a few lilies to calm himself. Glancing from time to time at the path, he sketched and waited.

'That's the first time I've seen a drawing of yours, you know.'

Adam turned, startled, and shut his pad. She always turned up from where you least expected it. As if she knew he was looking out for her.

Adam began to speak, but Laila shook her head and gently took the pad from him, opening it to the page he had just been sketching. Smiling with her eyes and her mouth, she pointed to herself. *For me?* Adam just nodded. Looking up, she asked for permission to look through the pad at his other drawings. Adam was reluctant. She'd probably think he was mad if she saw his scribblings and his random words and his worst fears. Because that's what it amounted to. His memory dump. Full of the worst of his fears and the best of his thoughts which weren't that good at all. Seeing him tense, Laila nodded and patted the pad.

'Another time then,' she said lightly.

He wanted to draw her fingers then. The way she fluttered them to say, *It's OK, it's cool, I understand, it's your stuff, your thing, I get it.* It wasn't quite signing like Farah did, but he could easily discern what she was trying to say. One flutter, many words and thoughts. Sitting near him, but not next to him Laila looked over the lily park and stared right ahead. Adam felt something new. He couldn't place it. He couldn't draw it, scribble it, write it or speak it. Then he realised what it was. It was the feeling of tranquillity. A light movement of Laila's fingers caught Adam's eye. Adam twitched to draw her fluttering butterfly fingers.

Butterfly. Better fly. Fly better. But to fly.

Grabbing his pad, he quickly sketched her fingers, two thumbs touching lightly in the middle, fingers in the shape of two butterfly wings. On the hands he drew swirling lily shapes swaying in the wind. He looked up from time to time to see the expression on her face. Smiling, she looked away and left her hands sitting on her lap, which was all he really needed.

There was blood on his hands, on his apron, on everything. Earlier he'd blown his nose and bits of dried blood had come out. Not his own blood of course. The blood, dried and dusty, clung to everything. Grabbing a mop, Adam set about trying to clean the place, sluicing the floor with hot water. Blood and water. That's what we're made up of, thought Adam.

Blood was still in the shop, cleaning out the last of the meat and packing it into freezers. Adam looked at the clock and wondered what Laila was doing. Wondered if she wondered about him. He hoped she wouldn't come to see him here. Under the strip light he felt exposed. As Adam put the mop away, he glanced at the carcasses hanging in the freezer room on wicked-looking hooks. They were stripped bare, cleaned out and gutted. Without blood and water to make them live. Without hearts. Blood appeared to inspect Adam's work. He produced five crinkly notes.

'You've done the best you could with what you've got. Can't argue with that. Bloodstains aren't meant to be washed away. See you tomorrow.'

Throwing off his apron and pocketing the cash, Adam left the shop quickly. Outside he took in deep gulps to get rid of the smell of blood and fresh meat. His fingers itched to get on with his work in the train yard, but he knew he couldn't, not tonight.

Farah sat at William's feet, fascinated by his watch, the visible moving inner parts. William remembered how his consultant Dr Desai had noticed his watch and commented that the movement in a Swiss watch made by a master watchmaker would surely be very similar to the way a heart worked. He had called it, 'a fist of mechanical bits, very much like a heart'. Looking at his watch, William agreed. It was the most expensive and finest thing he owned; in fact it was the only thing he owned, even his clothes were borrowed. The watch was the only item he was willing to be buried with. He didn't have any expectations about the afterlife, but he felt that waking up and not knowing the time would be annoying.

Was this watch a gift? signed Farah.

'No, I made it. I collected all the parts and put it together.'

Farah's eyes widened and she gave William a thumbs up. He had never been given a thumbs up before and he found himself beaming. Farah took the watch from William with great care, cupping both tiny hands to receive it. She looked at the inner workings,, eyes following the see-sawing wheel that kept the watch ticking.

It's beautiful. It makes me sleepy listening to the tick tock.

It had always been William's dream to be a master watchmaker. To travel to Switzerland and create some of the greatest watches in history. Unfortunately for William, nobody he knew shared his fascination for lugs and hands, cogs and jewels. Nobody believed in William so he stopped believing in himself. His fascination with time and clocks never dimmed, but he never reached the Swiss valleys. Instead William worked for a local jeweller, fixing broken clocks and watches. Most of the watches that came through the shop just needed a battery replaced or a little wind and a clean to get them going again. William lived for the moments when occasionally somebody would come into the shop with a mechanical watch. Usually an old watch they had inherited that they didn't know how to look after. With tender care and the gentlest of touches, William would bring the watch back to life. He would take the whole watch apart, cleaning every piece and oiling every cog. He would set each piece down on a white square of muslin and stare at the watch until he fixed into his brain how it had been tooled. Slowly, and with considerable patience, he would rebuild the watch, piecing it together, sometimes even fashioning new pieces where the old ones had been worn down. When the customer returned, William would enjoy their gasps at how the newly polished timepiece sparkled. A healthy, working watch, humming with life. His boss would say to him, 'Well, it's not quite Geneva, but at least the people in Guildford are getting to work on time.' William knew this wasn't really a compliment, but he didn't care and he waited each day for another mechanical watch, hoping it would be in a worse state of repair and more complicated than the last.

A little smile playing on her lips, Farah climbed into William's lap, and with the watch still pressed against her ear she leaned into William and nestled her other ear against his chest. Making herself comfortable, she tucked in her knees, closed her eyes and listened to the syncopated beating of the two heart-pieces. William could feel the thud of Farah's little heart. He brought his arms together to envelop her. He held Farah close to his chest and imagined her to be a fragile cog placed carefully in the centre wheel of his heart.

Adam threw his hands out in front to stop himself falling. He sat up with a start. Just a dream. He tried to jot down some of the fragments still tangled in his brain, but they escaped like water in a sieve; his mind was full of holes. The dream had been so vivid. Adam climbed out of bed to get a cool glass of water. It was still early evening and the house was quiet. Rubbing at his scratchy eyes, some more fragments of memory pinched at him then hid from sight. Adam drank deeply from his glass and settled his mind. He pushed open the door to the living room. The curtains were drawn and the room was almost pitch black. Waiting for his eyes to adjust, he stared at the armchair where a large shape sat unmoving.

'I don't remember falling asleep,' said William in a strange voice.

'Me neither,' replied Adam, yawning.

'I had such a strange dream,' yawned William in reply.

'Me too. Strange as.' Adam described bits of the dream that had left a residue in his brain.

'I had the same dream,' whispered William.

'What does that mean, that we both had the same dream? Does that mean something?'

William took a long while before replying. 'It means he's still here with us. I've had lots of dreams about him And thoughts, and bits of memory and sometimes snippets of conversation that I can't remember and think must be his. But I don't trust them. They can't be real. My mind must be creating them.'

'Yes, it must be our minds. Dadda gave his heart, not a brain. There's no hard drive in the heart.'

Adam realised that William was laughing.

'Why you laughing?'

'It's the way you describe things. Hard drive – very good.'

'It's funny . . . ?'

'No. It's full of . . . something. Full of images and clever. I wish I had such a way with words.'

'Why? You say little and that's enough.'

'I've spent my whole life saying little. Sometimes I wish I'd said a lot.'

'Why don't you?'

'I think it's because it was only ever me and my mum. She was always working, and when she was home she was too tired to speak or do anything.'

'What about the rest of your family?

'My mum raised me, but she died years ago. My dad was Irish. My mum was Jamaican. They met waiting at a bus stop, it was pouring with rain and dad covered mum with his jacket. She told me he was very charming, and not long after, she fell pregnant. Dad had been brought up as a strict Catholic, so they got married. He was in the navy and his dream was to buy a little boat and come back for us, but he never did. So she was stuck with me, a light-skinned baby with gingery brown hair and freckles. I was a daily reminder of him, and I looked nothing like her. It was hard for her having me. She had it hard and it made her hard . . .' William tailed off.

'Like my mum,' replied Adam.

'A bit. But your mum isn't hard with me.'

'Or with Farah. Just me.'

'Because she sees something in you. Something better.'

'I wish she'd tell me that. She never even looks at me. Ever since Dad left, she doesn't see me.'

'Just give her time. She'll talk to you when she's ready.'

'I thought my Dadda would talk to me too, when he was ready, but he never did. Maybe my mum won't either.'

'Give her time, Adam. She'll come around.'

'William, when you left after that first day you knocked on our door, I didn't think you'd come back. I was getting used to people leaving and never coming back. But you did, each day, and every time I thought you wouldn't. What I said before, when I was angry about my Dadda sending you to us as a cruel joke, I take it back. It's not a joke, it's good. It makes sense.'

William laughed out loud. 'Adam, I never thought I'd still be alive. Never thought I'd ever be a part of a family or make sense of my life. But here I am. I tell you what else doesn't make sense: I keep having these cravings for different foods and drink I've never had before.'

Adam smiled. 'I bet I know what you fancy right now . . . You're thinking, *I could murder a cup of hot chai.*'

'Do you mind if you add a pinch of masala for me too . . . ?'

The room exploded with warmth and energy as Adam and William set about making chai together, banishing the silence of the house.

Laila watched Adam leave school. He was so unusual, she thought. Unlike the others, Adam didn't wait around at the school gates to talk or amble home in a large group. Instead he would practically jog out of there. Almost as if he was running a race. Looping her bag over her shoulder, she stepped up her pace in case she lost him. She liked looking at him. Face all angles and cheekbones, giving him a glowering look, like he was annoyed all the time. But he wasn't, she knew he wasn't, and although she told no one else this, when he looked at her his eyes changed. They didn't glower, they seemed to glow. She couldn't look into them for too long. They were so full of fire, and when he looked at her they filled with something else. Need. *Stop it or you'll lose him!* Keeping her eyes on his rucksack, she remembered how they had first met. It had been in the school canteen. One of those days when the rain finds a way into your bones no matter what you do. Everybody had trudged into school and every available space had been sat on, stood in, staked out. She had been dripping, her thick hair sodden and flat against her scalp and her feet squelching in her shoes. She had been miserable. And, thinking about it, not looking her best. Having nowhere to sit, she had dragged her feet to a patch of floor near a radiator. Like pulling the string and drawing a curtain, the crowd had parted to let her pass and a space had emerged. It usually did when she appeared somewhere. They called her a witch because of her wild hair, and from the start she had done her best to cultivate the image. Everybody had moved away except him. The boy with the burning eyes. He had stayed exactly where he was. Again, doing what she had least expected. Sitting down and wringing out her hair, she had sat with her knees tucked in, damp clothes sticking to her skin. Laila had noticed him of course, but was in no mood to talk. As she sat, drying off, she could feel his eyes staring at her, almost a match for the heat from the radiator.

'What?' she had asked without turning to face him.

'I didn't say anything.'

'You're staring at me as if you want to though.'

'How would you know? You're not even looking at me.'

Seeing this as a direct challenge, she turned to look and was confronted by the boy's strange angular face and sharp cheekbones and that glower. The crackling embers in his eyes, his shock of jet-black hair . . .

'Now who's staring . . . ?'

Embarrassed, she broke eye contact and bit the inside of her cheek.

They went back to staring straight ahead in a more

companionable silence. Both alone with their thoughts, but no longer as lonely as they had been a moment ago. The space between them had been filled with words, looks and eyes. And awkwardness.

'You have strange eyes,' he had said after a long moment.

Misunderstanding the comment as a challenge, a criticism, she was about to fire something back. Something suitably witch-like, to suit her image, but something in his voice stopped her. It hadn't been said in a negative way. It was said with curiosity.

'What's so strange about them?' she asked.

'They seem to be two different colours. Depending on the light. Green and grey.'

'I've always just thought they were green. Light green.'

'No. When you're a little bit angry, they turn grey. Like storm clouds.'

Continuing to bite the inside of her mouth, she had wanted to smile. What an unusual boy. She had turned to him then, and shuffled a little closer. Then, bravely, she had stared him full in the face.

'What colour are they now then?'

'Sea green. With ripples of grey. But the ripples, they seem to be calm now, not as angry as they were.'

The bell had gone then, and a thousand damp, cold bodies had trudged to their next lesson. All except the girl who only a few short moments ago had been cold to the bone but was now warmed by the fire in the boy's eyes, and the boy who had not moved.

* * *

Admonishing herself again for such distracting thoughts, Laila tried her best to close the gap between her and Adam. He had arrived at what seemed to be a large industrial park and was walking around the wall as if looking for something. Suddenly he had ducked and disappeared from sight. Swearing, she sped up, but couldn't find where he had gone. That's typical of him, she thought. After all that, he just disappears. Then, looking closely, she found a grille of some sort. It had been moved slightly. Unless you were standing right over it, you wouldn't see it. What would he be doing in there? Doing what you least expect of course. She toyed with the idea of sneaking up on him and surprising him, but thought that would probably spook him. He had a few secrets, but that was OK, so did everyone. She would wait until he was ready to share. She had convinced herself that she had followed him because she was worried about him. But, standing there, she'd realised that she was curious and a little bit annoyed that he would rush off and not talk with her. But she would wait, until he was ready, until the time was right.

Adam arrived home to find two big men standing outside his house. Yasmin stood on the threshold, hands on hips and chin jutting out. She was putting on a brave face, but Adam could tell she was shaken. The men, hands in pockets, breathed power. Physical and nasty. As he came closer, he recognised them from around the ends, two local tough lads known as Brick and Block. Adam walked up to them.

'What is it?'

Turning to him slowly, they smiled and then laughed.

'Ah, this must be the man of the house. All right, boy.'

'What do you want?'

'We was just telling your mum that your grandpa – our condolences by the way – had a nasty habit of losing money. And although we're sorry he's dead an all that, this is his, as you would say, registered address.'

Adam's mind spun. Dadda would never gamble. He just wasn't a gambler. Or was he? Looking at his mum frowning, she was clearly thinking the same thing. He hadn't told us about the heart – what else hadn't he told us about?

'He didn't gamble,' said Adam.

'We have slips and signatures to say he did.'

'But he's gone, and we can't pay. We haven't got the money.'

The bigger man turned to Adam and took a step to tower over him.

'Now, as you are the man of the house, and because of the circumstances, we're going to take a lenient view. So we're going to give you a bit of time.'

'But he's gone—'

'Now, come on, behave. I was talking,' the bigger man cut in, voice dangerously low. He continued.

'You have some time. Not a lot, but some. Now, I'm sure you'll have our money very soon, but if you don't, we'll be having more than words.' He said this last looking at both Adam and then pointedly at Yasmin. The two men were like two blocks of iron. Coarse and rough and hard. As the man towered over him, Adam stood his ground. His stomach was churning, but he wasn't so scared of the men or the damage they could do to him. He was scared of the damage they could do to his mum and Farah. The big man knew this. This was his business. But when he next spoke, there was a grudging respect.

'Not scared are you, son?'

'No,' replied Adam, looking into the man's dark eyes.

'Well, no reason to be, is there, if you do what we ask. It's simple really.'

The bigger man held out his hand for Adam to shake. Adam looked at the thick, gnarled fingers. Scars crisscrossed across the knuckles, they were like shanks of pulped meat. They had inflicted pain and felt pain. Adam refused to shake the hand.

'Got a bit of fizz in you, lad. That's good, that's all good,' said the man, bunching his hand into a fist. 'Shows heart.'

Involuntarily, Adam laughed. *Your heart is the size of your clenched fist.* This man's heart would be huge. And ugly.

The man looked at Adam strangely and glanced at his partner, slightly uncertain. After living with his dad's abuse for so long, Adam had realised a few things about bullies. That if you stopped fearing them, no matter how big or strong they were, they lost their hold over you.

The other man walked past Adam, still trying to stare him down.

'We'll be back.'

Adam turned to watch them go and blew out a long breath, deflating his lungs of pent-up tension. Yasmin put a protective hand on his shoulder. It was the first time she'd touched him for so long.

'I thought he was going to smack you when you started to laugh.'

'Yeah, he had a dark look in his eye.'

'I can't believe Dadda owed any money to anyone.'

'No, but we need to make sure, because they'll be back.'

'It doesn't seem right.'

'No, none of it seems right,' agreed Adam. Lifting her hand from his shoulder, Yasmin turned back into the house. Adam stayed and watched the two blots stride down the street until they turned a corner and were gone.

* * *

Yasmin stroked Farah's cheek, giving her a tired smile. Adam stopped in front of her.

'Did you see that?' asked Adam. He had seen the curtain twitch and knew she'd been watching.

Yes. Bad men?

'Very bad men.'

What do they want?

'Money.'

We haven't got any money.

'That's what I told them.'

Will they come back?

'Maybe.'

I gave them my worst evil eye.

'That really bad one that you do?'

Yeah, my worst, evillest one.

'Then they probably won't come back.'

Farah had seen enough of the two men to know that they were bad. She knew that because of the way they had stood and the way they had kept their hands in their pockets. But most of all she knew because of the way they had smiled. They had smiled for the sake of smiling, not because they had wanted to. Farah had watched her brother too. She was always watching him. He was often hunched over, as if his rucksack had heavy rocks in it. He didn't look up at the sky or look ahead. He looked down. When they went to the park, she would always prod him. *Look up! Look up!* He would smile and humour her, but then look down again. She could tell he wasn't scared of the men, but he was frightened by what they could do. She

116

considered going out there and thumping the men over the heads with her big book until they went away and wouldn't come back, but thought her mum would get upset.

Adam picked Farah up and squeezed her tight. She put her arms around his neck and held him close. Like a parent comforting a child, Farah patted Adam and stroked his back. Setting her down, Adam crossed his arms over his chest and pointed at her. Smiling, Farah took two fingers and pointed to her eyes and pointed at her brother. He had taught her it, telling her, *I'm watching you.* Now she was telling him the same. Seeing a smile on his face, a genuine smile, Farah was pleased. Crossing her arms, she pointed to him and waved. Still smiling, he waved back.

Where's William?

'I don't know.'

He's usually here for tea.

'I'm sure he'll be back later. Don't worry so much about him.'

Farah thought she'd go and spend some time with her book. William would soon be back in the moss-green chair.

Yasmin marched into the room and tapped Farah on the shoulder.

'Right, you two, I need some bits for dinner. Here's the list, William. Farah will show you where and what.'

William stood up uncertainly and looked at Farah then at Yasmin.

'Don't look so pleased about it. I need to give this room a good clean.'

She gave William some money.

'She likes to skip ahead, and sometimes she doesn't concentrate when crossing the road. I need you to hold her hand. OK?'

William looked down at Farah, who was hopping from foot to foot ready to go, and back up at Yasmin and nodded firmly.

'OK.'

Farah held out her hand, and William, looking at her little fingers, enveloped it in his large paw. Farah signalled that it was too tight, scrunching up her face. William slackened a little but still held on tight as they set out. Farah skipped, matching William's long stride as they ambled down the street in the crisp air. William looked about him at the lively streets. There were people sitting on their steps chatting to friends and neighbours. Others sat in cars listening to music while a few boys kicked a ball across the street. He didn't know this place and these people. Yet somehow he felt a closeness he couldn't explain and a sense of belonging he had never had before. A sense of belonging that was not his. As they walked, William felt eyes on him, on Farah. Eyes that looked and then quickly darted away. Farah yanked on his arm and signed, *This is fun*, and skipped along, leading him towards the shops. Then she led William around the shop, filling their basket, working her way through the list. Pointing to a packet of chocolate digestives, Farah gave William the thumbs up. *I know you like these!* Looking down at the list, William didn't see chocolate digestives anywhere. Frowning, he followed Farah around the aisles, putting things back that weren't on the list. Finally arriving at the counter, Farah smiled sweetly at the shopkeeper and pointed.

'How are you, child? Do you want your usual?'

118

Farah nodded and held out her hand. Reaching behind him, the man produced a handful of liquorice sweets. Farah cupped her hands and stuffed the sweets in her coat pocket. Nodding and smiling, the old man reached down and patted Farah on the head. Then he saw William and his face changed.

'Who are you, and what are you doing with her?'

William thought about the question. Where could he possibly start?

'I . . . I'm a friend of the family,' he replied eventually.

'A friend?'

'Yes. A sort of relative.' William regretted the words as soon as he had said them.

'You, a relative? I've never seen you before.'

Farah grabbed William's hand and waved at the old shopkeeper.

He's with me.

The shopkeeper looked at William with even more suspicion.

'What did she say?'

'She said, "He's with me." How much do we owe you?'

Unconvinced, the shopkeeper took the money from William, still staring at him. Farah dragged William out of the shop and into the street. She pulled him along by the arm as other people turned to stare at them. William allowed himself to be led away from the scrutiny of many sets of eyes and he lost all sense of direction until they arrived at the park. He blinked.

'What are we doing here?'

We're going to the park.

'I think we should go home. Your mum will be waiting.'

Letting go of William's hand, Farah made a face and sighed. She signed irritably.

'OK, OK, we can go to the park for a few minutes.'

Grabbing his hand once again, Farah led William to the adventure playground and skipped off towards the climbing frames. William spotted an empty bench from where he could see Farah wherever she was. Setting the shopping down, he slumped down heavily. There were a number of other kids on the slides and swings being watched by their parents, but William was glad they were on the other side, away from him. Farah leaped onto the climbing frame and made easy work of each obstacle. She had no fear of falling and the joy on her face as she climbed higher or jumped from one post to the next made William want to applaud. Daringly at the top of the climbing frame, Farah hung by one hand and waved at William with the other. Nervously William waved back, willing her to put her other hand back on the bar. Just as he was standing up to help Farah in case she fell, he felt a hand on his shoulder.

'Excuse me, sir, could we have a word, please?'

William turned to see two police officers.

'What about?'

'If we could just step out of this area, sir . . .'

William glanced over his shoulder to where Farah was still climbing.

'We've had some complaints that you've been harassing the Shah family. Turning up every day unannounced. So if you could just follow us, I'm sure we can clear this up right away.'

'I'm not harassing them. I'm sort or . . . erm . . . part of their family.'

Another look passed between the officers, and one of them nodded.

'I'm afraid we're going to have to insist that you come with us. We don't want a fuss, not in front of the children. So, please, just come along and you can tell us all about it away from here.'

William turned to Farah and, catching her eye, waved, beckoning her to join him.

'What are you doing?'

'I'm proving to you that I'm part of the family,' replied William.

'Stop waving, put your arm down now. Sir. Do it now or we'll have to arrest you.'

'Let me prove it to y—'

One of the police officers clamped a handcuff around William's free hand while the other grabbed his other. William didn't struggle, just turned to see Farah running towards him. Signing frantically, Farah ran alongside the police officers. *What are you doing? Let him go? He's with me! He's with me!*

One of the police officers fell back and stood in front of Farah while the other pushed William into the back of their police car.

'It's OK. Go back and play now. We'll deal with it. Go on.'

The officer gave her a gentle nudge back in the direction of the park. Farah stumbled and watched in horror as both police officers slammed their doors shut and sped off.

William sat in the detention cell staring at the grimy door. His thoughts a jumble, he tried to bring some order to his mind. Hooking his right hand over his left shoulder and across his heart, he rocked back and forth on the edge of the bench. He had suddenly realised in the police car how his being in the park would have looked to the policemen, and to the other parents. He had tried his best to explain why he had been there, and even to his ears he had found the words odd. He had realised then how fantastical it sounded. How outrageous. How irregular. *I'm part of the family.* The police officer had looked at him, as if to say, *What are you talking about?* It made him ask himself what was he doing. What did he want from this family? Could he give them anything? What was he, now that this heart was not his?

He remembered lying in his bed, not long after the operation, feeling drowsy and being aware of the doctor examining him. His eyes had been closed, but he had been listening to the conversation between the two surgeons.

'He seems to be doing well, even if it feels like he looks a bit sad about it all,' said Dr Desai.

'Yes, all points to a regular recovery. You say he has no family to speak of?' replied Dr Herrick.

'None that I know or was ever mentioned. What a strange quirk of fate that the very heart our Mr Tide needed was beating across from him the whole time.'

'And what a fascinating donor Mr Abdul-Aziz Shah was. He said very little, and was adamant it had to be his heart, and only that.'

'Well, he did a good thing, and now another gets to live in his stead and that's what matters,' replied Dr Desai.

Unstrapping his watch, William stared as the second hand swept around the numbers. He should never have heard that conversation. He was hanging on to the Shah family. Using them to heal. Using them for his own selfish reasons. Using their kindness against them. They had already been through a lot, been used a lot. William sat back and leaned against the wall. Strapping his watch back on to his wrist, he knew what he had to do. Once the police let him go, William would leave the Shah family alone. Alone to grieve and alone to live. Having made his decision, he let the anchor drag him down into the deep, black darkness of his old heart. The heart that was no good.

Yasmin, Adam and Farah waited at the police-station reception, trying to be patient. Farah held on to Adam's fingers while Yasmin tapped her index finger on the desk. The police officer folded his arms and looked at her. Farah could tell he was not impressed.

'How many times do I have to tell you? He's with us,' said Yasmin.

'I appreciate that, Mrs Shah . . .'

'It's "Miss".'

'Miss Shah. But there was a complaint.'

'What complaint?'

'I can't go into the details of that, but we need to investigate it properly before we can let him out.'

'I told you that I sent him with my daughter, Farah. I gave him some money to get some shopping and they must have decided to go to the park. You decided to arrest him, and you left my daughter – a child – behind, to come home alone, distressed. What else do you need to know?'

'It's not as simple as that. There was a complaint.'

'Complaint from who?'

'People from the community, friends of yours.'

Adam glanced at his mum and saw flames in her eyes. She was about to explode and the whole police station would be ablaze. Putting a hand on her arm to calm her, Adam spoke in a softer voice to the now frowning police officer.

'Look, William is not whatever you think he might be. He's not a criminal and he shouldn't be here. Unless you're going to charge him with something, let us take him home.'

'We received a complaint, and we're just trying to get to the bottom of this situation.'

Yasmin blew out a hot gust of air and was about to start flaming the police officer when Farah yanked on her fingers. Signing deliberately, Farah looked up at the police officer and pointed to herself. The anger dissipated from both the officer and Yasmin as they watched her.

'What did she say?' asked the officer with weary resignation.

Adam put a hand on Farah's shoulder and squeezed it.

'She said that what you're doing isn't right. William hasn't done anything wrong, and going to the park was her idea. She said that he was good even if he was a little quiet, but that she was quiet too and if being quiet meant someone was a little odd or weird, then there would be lots of people in jail. That maybe then you should put her in jail too, because she didn't like to talk much either. She also said that he had come to us, and that it wasn't easy for him to have come but he did, and that was important and that's why he was with us. That he belonged to us. She said you don't look like a mean man, she can tell by your eyes, and all that frowning is just an act, and that you understand really and that you know what we're saying is true.'

The police officer leaned over the desk to get a better look at the little girl.

'She said all that?'

'Yes. And for her that's a lot.'

Looking from face to face, the police officer nodded. 'OK. I can see this means a lot to you. And that even if it's a bit . . . irregular, there's been no crime committed. Wait here and I'll go and find out what's going on.'

The Shahs watched as the officer disappeared into another room to talk to someone. Adam looked across at his mum, still sitting on the edge of her chair, eyes still blazing. The police officer returned and sat back down. Although he still looked serious, his eyes were gentler, especially when he looked at Farah.

'OK, I've had a word and we've run some checks. It all seems clear. Please go back to the waiting room and he will be processed and come out there soon.'

Farah signed to Adam, *Are you sure they'll let him go?*

Nodding, Adam replied. *They promised.*

Accompanied by the police officer, William looked dishevelled, confused and surprised to see the three of them waiting for him. Farah was the first to skip to him and hug his leg. Adam came forward to shake his hand and Yasmin gently squeezed his shoulder. William felt such warmth for them then, and joy that they had come for him. But even in that moment, he knew that as much as he didn't want to, as much as his new heart told him to stay, his old heart told him to leave. They all walked out of the station together, but William was already thinking of ways to be alone.

Laila watched as Adam set about sketching. They were sitting in the art room at lunchtime and were alone except for Mrs Matheson, who was getting the room ready for the afternoon lesson. It was quiet but for the scratching of Adam's pencil on the white sheet. They had agreed to meet and do their work together, but she had done nothing – she couldn't stop herself from watching Adam as he drew. He was fully immersed in the movement of the pencil, his eyes never leaving the page, his focus and intensity burning the graphite onto the white sheet. She noted the way he sat, hunched over, close to the page almost as if he wanted to lean right into whatever he was sketching.

'It's strange, isn't it?'

Laila started and turned to see Mrs Matheson at her shoulder.

'He works with total concentration. Like there's nothing else here.'

'He looks like he's in a trance.'

'In a way, I suppose he is,' she agreed. 'He's living inside his work. It's . . . wonderful to see.'

Laila turned to look at Mrs Matheson. She saw excitement and pride in her eyes. Adam wasn't her best student, or the most talented, but she saw something in him. 'Do you see? He feels it. He really feels it. That's what makes a real artist.'

'Why does he sit funny when he's drawing?'

Mrs Matheson sat down next to Laila and smiled.

'It's not directly in front of him . . .' continued Laila.

'No. It's turned to the side, almost upside down. It's such an awkward angle to draw at, but still he manages to use it to his advantage. I think it's the way his mind works, the way he deals with things. Positioning the paper so it's almost uncomfortable is his way of making it difficult.'

'Why make it difficult? Why not make it easier?'

She looked at Laila with gentle eyes.

'Because that's his way of getting to the answers he needs. That's his way of seeing.'

'I'm not sure I understand.'

'No, it's not clear to me either what goes through his head,' replied Mrs Matheson, and walked away, smiling to herself.

Laila went back to studying the dark-haired boy engrossed in his work. She'd never looked at a boy before. Not in the way she looked at *him*. But even now she wasn't sure what he was thinking. Every time she looked into his eyes, whatever fire consumed him burnt any evidence that he was there with her. And yet she wanted to sit with him, would have liked to hold his hand, trace the sharp edges of his cheekbones with her fingers and hold him. Tell him that he was OK. That it was OK. Laila understood that Adam was trying to reshape the world. Trying to redraw it the way he saw it.

'You bored?' asked Adam from across the room.

'No. It's nice being here in the silence.'

'A bit dull though, isn't it?'

Laila shook her head.

'Don't do that.'

'Do what?' asked Adam.

'Try to get rid of me. Push me away.'

'I wasn't. I was just saying, life's a bit dull with me at times.'

'You can be distant, but I don't mind that. Because when you speak, you've thought about what you're saying.'

Putting down his pencil, Adam puffed out his cheeks and stared at Laila. He knew he was staring. He knew she knew he was staring. But this time he didn't care. The light in the art room was better than in any of the other classrooms in the school. Large rectangular windows and high ceilings that let you see the sky. Adam had often wondered whether you could draw at all if you couldn't see the sky. His eye caught the light behind Laila, making her look unearthly.

'Now you're being quiet and staring,' she said.

'I know. It's the light behind you. It's so . . .'

'I know. It's the huge windows, the light in here is beautiful. It—'

'I wasn't staring at the light and thinking it was beautiful.'

'Oh,' replied Laila, looking at her hands suddenly, as Adam stopped staring and studied the writing on his pencil.

'Farah, my little sister, she likes sitting in the light too. Helps her think,' said Adam, breaking the silence.

'I'd love to meet her. You said that she was quiet too?'

131

'Very quiet, in some ways. She had an . . . accident, and ever since that . . . happened she doesn't speak. But she's not a quiet one,' replied Adam. Seeing Laila's confused look, he smiled. 'Hard to explain.'

'Is there anything about you that isn't?'

'It's a good line to use when you don't want to talk about something. "Hard to explain" – and then shrug your shoulders. William does it all the time . . .'

'Who's William?'

Laila watched as Adam shifted in his seat and looked down at his drawing.

'Erm, hard to explain?' He replied, grinning.

Laila smiled back. 'You don't have to tell me, Adam. It's OK, I get it. You don't have to tell me everything right now.'

'I want to tell you. I'm going to tell you, one day,' replied Adam, looking Laila in the eye again.

Nothing about his life made sense. Farah not speaking, a guy called William as part of their family, where his dad was . . . But this, sitting here with her, made a lot of sense.

She said nothing. Adam noticed her slender fingers were resting on the table. He wondered how her fingers would look entwined with his. Grabbing his pencil, he snapped it in two. The snap made Laila start. Walking around the table, she took his hands in hers, and took the broken pencil from him.

'Promise me you'll never break another pencil again. You look so beautiful when you draw, like the world has stopped and there is only you and the scratch of your pencil. I could watch you all day. Promise me.'

'I promise,' replied Adam, trembling. 'I don't know where to begin with all of it. There's so much.'

'No. It isn't too much, it's your life. I want to help.'

'You do help. In so many ways. So much that it's . . .'

'Hard to explain?' replied Laila, a smile tugging at her lips.

When Mrs Matheson walked back into the room, she was surprised and pleased to see two silhouetted figures holding hands. But what really made her smile and edge back out of the doorway was to see that the room that was so full of light was, for this afternoon at least, so full of laughter.

Adam stood in the middle of the ward. Looking down, he saw that he was in a pale green hospital gown. His feet were bare. It was dark but for the light from the corridor. A racking cough cut the silence and Adam felt his heart quicken. What was he doing here? The thrumming in his chest made him feel queasy. A few shafts of moonlight shot through the window behind him, bathing some of the patients, reminding Adam of a prison spotlight searching out escapees. Perhaps those the light fell upon were marked in some way. Adam now remembered why he called it the death ward. You could taste death on the tip of your tongue, and the sense of helplessness was palpable. Adam held out his hands in front of him. They weren't his hands. They were old hands. Wrinkled, gnarled, nut brown. He put these hands up to feel his face and he felt hair, a short beard around and under his cheeks. What was going on?

'Now, now, what's gone on here? Do you need the toilet, love?'

Adam looked up to see a short, stocky nurse striding towards him.

'What?'

'Do you need the toilet? I can get the bedpan, or if you're up to it, I can help you to the loo?'

'No, I'm OK. What am I doing here?' asked Adam, heart thumping now.

'Come on, lovey, you're a bit confused. It's past midnight. Let's get you to bed, eh.'

'I'm not supposed to be here. I'm not ill.'

'That's what they all say. Sorry, ducky, but you are a bit ill. Come on, back into bed.'

Adam planted his legs and stood firm.

The nurse looked at him and patiently nodded her head.

'OK, ducky, OK.'

'What's my name . . . ?'

'Poor love. Look, let's get you into bed so you can rest . . .'

'Please. Tell me my name,' pleaded Adam.

The nurse sighed and held up her hands.

'Your name, sweetheart, is Abdul-Aziz. Abdul-Aziz Shah.'

Swaying, Adam held onto the frame of the bed and steadied himself.

'That's not me. That's not my name.'

The nurse pressed a button near the bed, and a few seconds later another nurse appeared. Together they began to gently lift Adam into the bed. Adam wanted to fend them off, wanted to move, wanted to run. But all he could do was helplessly push against the nurses. They swaddled him in sheets and tucking him in secured his weak limbs to the bed.

'There you go, ducky. Now, you get some good rest, and no more walkabout, you hear. I'll come by to check on you shortly.'

Adam watched as the two nurses bustled out of the ward, chattering with one another. He was stuck fast. Something was digging into him. Adam reached underneath his side. Feeling something there, he pulled until it came away and was in his hands. He knew what the object was. His Dadda's prayer beads. He used the last of his strength to pull himself up. He remembered his Dadda sitting in his armchair flicking the beads and staring out of the window. He'd often thought that praying helped his Dadda to relax. Just as drawing helped Adam to feel calm. Adam pushed the beads, one after the other, and felt a tranquillity that helped compose him. The beads were textured and rough to the touch. Bringing them up to his nose, Adam smelt them. A shock of scents assailed his nose and thoughts of his Dadda flooded into his head. His grandfather had always smelt of smoke and sandalwood. His thick green cable-knit cardigan hoarding a mix of musty scents. Adam remembered rushing downstairs each morning to sit in his lap and drink milk. His Dadda wouldn't say anything, just point to the glass and nod. After Adam had drained his glass, his Dadda would point to the remains of the moustache the milk had left behind and nod again. Adam would wipe the milk off with the back of his hand and hop off and away. When he shook his head to dislodge one memory, another took its place. This time walking into a stationer's and wondering at all the different pens and pencils and pads and paper all around him. His Dadda had only come in to buy some envelopes, but seeing Adam's fascination had followed his eyes and bought him his first set of pencils. No colour, perhaps he had not been ready for colour just then, but different grades of grey. He remembered gripping that box of pencils in both hands and rushing home to draw something, anything. He tried his best to remember what he had drawn first, but it escaped him. Still fingering the beads, Adam forced his eyes open and tried to clear his head. What was he doing here?

'Adam. Are you awake?'

'William . . . ? What am I doing here?'

'Where else are you supposed to be?'

'I . . . don't know, but not here.'

'Adam, I have to tell you something. I have to go.'

'Go where? What are you talking about?'

'I have to go away. I shouldn't have come. You have enough to deal with, and I don't need to add to that.'

'Away? You can't, William. You came to us, remember? You can't just leave. They both left. My dad, Dadda. All my fathers. Not you too.'

'If I stay, it will complicate things for all of you. You don't need me to remind you of what you've lost. I'm making it difficult for you with your community. If I'm not there, you can all get on with your lives.'

Flicking the beads at a furious rate, Adam stared at William. This wasn't happening. This couldn't be happening. This was just a . . . dream.

The sensation was one of falling again as Adam woke. The clammy bed-sheets stuck to him. Kicking them off, Adam sat up in bed. Every bit of that dream had felt real. He had been his Dadda in the death ward. He had felt and smelt and touched everything. He had spoken to William, and William had said he was leaving. Adam knew then that it was more than just a dream.

He ran down the stairs, taking the steps two at a time, and barged into the living room. It was empty. He had left William there a few hours ago, sitting in the armchair, a blanket tucked around him and a cup of tea at his side. Climbing into the armchair and pulling the discarded blanket around him, Adam wept.

Adam stood looking out at the closely packed trains. It was dark, and hard to see clearly, but the quiet helped, with the monotony of what he was doing, made him feel at peace with himself. Flexing his fingers, Adam carried on spraying the strips of metal. The minute he stopped, rogue thoughts would rush into his head. Thoughts about his dad, his mum, his granddad, William, Farah, Laila, everyone. Thoughts and images, words and letters, faces and clocks and hearts and everything. Until he blinked hard and shook the jumble of thoughts out of his head. Pressing down on the spray-can nozzle, Adam continued to cover his world in blood-red paint. Covering up the cracks in the grey metal strips. But there was one thought he could not dislodge. Adam dreaded the idea of meeting up with his dad. He had arranged it so hastily at the time. He had said yes to get rid of him, to make him go away. And now he was seeing him again. For what? So he could tell him to get lost? Go away? Like William? Adam slumped down on the very edge of the train roof, his back to the drop below. He felt as if he was at the edge of an abyss. Looking over his shoulder was like looking into a well. Your eyes played tricks on you, making you see the bottom, but the darkness was unfathomable. Adam leaned back a little bit more. What if he closed his eyes and fell into it? Would he keep falling forever, watching as all the parts and people of his life rushed by? It would be so easy to just lean back and . . .

'Yo! Adam? You up here?'

Tank's voice echoed eerily round the yard. Sitting up, Adam composed himself and stuffed his rucksack with his spray cans.

'Yep. Wassup?' he replied.

'There's some kind of guard patrolling on the other side. He looks like he might come up here. Thought I'd warn you.'

Adam climbed down and jumped off the train, making his way over to Tank.

'Thanks. Just finishing anyway.'

'You almost done?'

Adam shrugged. 'Still got a bit to do.'

'You can't do it simple and tag a small patch of wall like the rest of us . . .' said Tank, grinning.

'It's just something that came to me. I don't know if it's a tag or anything . . .'

'It's a giant tag. A giant statement.'

'I don't know, man. It's just an idea.'

'I've seen you spray, cuz, and draw. You could be big on this scene if you wanted. But you're always alone and apart. You have to try to belong to something. Or else these other crews will dump your work. They'll think you too arrogant. You get me?'

'I'm not arrogant, just like to keep myself to myself. What's wrong with that?'

141

'Nuttin, man, I'm just sayin,' replied Tank, holding up his hands.

'So what's stopping them dumpin my work now then? I've done bits around – it's still up there. And this piece, some crews must know about it . . .'

'What you think's stopping them?'

'I don't know, Tank man, I just do my thing . . .'

Tank looked at Adam and smiled.

Adam stopped what he was saying and blurted, 'You? You're stopping them?'

'Why you think your skinny ass hasn't been kicked yet?'

'Because of you . . .' replied Adam in genuine surprise.

'Well, kind of. Because of me and Strides.'

'Strides? He don't even like me too much.'

'He don't talk too much, but he's been up there and seen your work. Seen what you're trying to do. That's enough for him. And me.'

'Enough for what?'

'For us to say you're part of our crew, fam. That you with us. The other crews won't dump you or your work, ya understand? Or mans will get touched, you get me.'

'Man, Tank, I don't know what to say . . .'

'Don't say nuttin, cuz. Don't want you to get too chatty now, do we? It'll do my head in.' Tank slapped Adam on the back. 'Come on, let's get out of here. Don't think that security guard is one of your fans.'

Walking back together, Adam stopped on the other side of the wall and held out his hand.

'Thanks, bruv. Means a lot.'

Tank grinned and, clasping his hand, he pulled Adam into an embrace. 'Man, look around you. We don't have too much to keep us occupied. It's not pretty here. If we don't respect the talent in ourselves, what else we got? You wanna be a roadman? One of those chiefs teefing man's goods? One of those wasteman robbing grannies on the high street? What else we got? We can draw, man, we have ideas about shape and colour, we can make a statement, ya understan? Who knows more about colour than us? Us that live in this black-and-white world. No need for thanks, bruv. Be true to the talent. Stay in school, drop out of school, but keep the pencil and the can close.'

Adam looked at the short, stocky figure of Tank. He had liked him the minute he had met him. Now he knew why. There was something earthy about him, like a tree root.

'OK, let's go. I feel like Malcolm X or sumthin, all inspirational an that. Might start keeping a memoir of me thoughts,' Tank said, chuckling.

'I'd want to read that,' replied Adam.

Looking sidelong at him, Tank burst out laughing.

'You too serious, man. Everything don't need to have *tone*! Some tings are just meant to be enjoyed.' Slapping Adam on the back once more, Tank threw a fist into the air and walked off up the road.

Tank's words swirled around Adam's head as he went to meet his dad. *Keep the pencil and the can close.* Adam smiled as he thought of Tank as a wise old stump with a unique way with words. *Be true to the talent.* Adam had never thought of what he had as talent. It was just something he could do. He could replicate most of anything he could see. That's not talent, is it? That's being a parrot, thought Adam. A dim memory nudged at him. Something Miss Matheson had once said. *'You're able to draw people's faces easily enough, a lot of people can. But you're able to capture something about them that reveals something to us. Even if that thing is grotesque or beautiful or bland, instinctively you're able to see it and show it. I can't teach you that, Adam. Nobody can. You either have it or you don't. If you carry on in this way, if you keep drawing and painting and learning about the world and about yourself, then maybe you'll recognise it in yourself one day.'*

Adam thought about the man he was going to meet. The man who had been his father, but was now, in his eyes, just another man. Adam had a rough idea as to how a father was supposed to be. And his dad came up short at best. Each flash of memory was painful. Every remembered snippet of conversation was angry and agonising. All the blows, each one hard and hurtful. They had lived apart from his Dadda and Daddima back then, just a few streets over. But the distance had been as wide as a canyon. As time went by, Adam had learned to read the signs, had known how to prepare, had found where to hide. But that made Adam angry with himself, that he had hidden when his mum couldn't. Or wouldn't. He had blamed her then. For not hiding, for not backing down, for making him feel embarrassed that he couldn't protect her. He was just a kid. What was he supposed to do? His mum had taken the blows, absorbing them into herself like a sponge, but

Adam knew she had cried the tears too. Angry tears squeezed out through a clenched fist.

Adam walked to the butcher's and waited outside. Blood waved and beckoned him in.

'You're early? It's only four thirty.'

'I'm meeting someone,' replied Adam, looking at his feet.

'Who?'

'My dad,' replied Adam.

'Oh. OK.'

'What?'

'Nothing. A boy needs his dad, even if he is a *goonda*. You know . . . we were close once, when we were about your age. He's not changed. Never wanted to work at anything, or build anything. Always wanted to cheat.'

'When did you stop being friends?'

Blood looked up at Adam and grimaced as he threw a large rack of meat onto the chopping board.

'When I decided that cheating life wouldn't get me anywhere. I understood that early on. Your dad never did. That's when we drifted apart.'

Nodding, Adam walked out of the shop. His dad was waiting for him on the kerb outside. Adam stiffened as his father gave him an awkward hug, a cigarette burning in his left hand.

'How are you, son? Look at your hair – it's all over the place. If your Dadda was here, he'd be at you to get it cut.'

'But he's not around.' *And neither are you*, Adam thought.

'No, true. Where shall we go? Burger and chips?'

'Yeah, OK, but I have to be back here by six.'

'Here?' replied Adam's dad, looking up at the butcher's shop.

'Yeah, I work here every day at six, cleaning up.'

'You don't need to work. I can give you money, Adam. You don't need to work for him. What's he paying you anyway? In lamb chops?' He chuckled to himself.

'He pays me enough,' Adam said.

'Yeah, well, watch him. He's sly, that one.' Funny, he said *you* were a cheat, thought Adam.

Adam walked with his father along the road to the takeaway and watched his dad while he joked with the man behind the counter as he ordered their food. Adam's dad knew everybody. He was well liked. People stopped him in the streets to say hello, have a chat. He was charming and told little jokes and made people smile. Adam wanted to scream at him, *Tell them about your life!* Or better still, let me tell them what it's like to be your son! How could his dad be two different people? He remembered the times his father would be out there on the streets waving to people, laughing and joking, and as soon as he had walked through the front door he would change into a glowering, difficult and angry man. A dark cloud followed him about. His face changed, his body became rigid and tense as a plank, and his fists . . . Adam always remembered his balled fists. *The size of your heart* . . . He had felt the size of his dad's heart. It was a ball of iron. Collecting their food, Adam's dad led them across the road to the park. They sat down on a bench and began to eat. Through mouthfuls, Adam's dad asked questions about school, home, Farah, even Yasmin.

'How's your mum? Is she OK after Dadda dying? Doing OK?' Adam looked at his dad. He noticed the concerned look, a little frown, lips pursed to show he cared. Head bobbing like those dogs at the back of cars. How did he do it? Was he that much of an actor that he could just turn it on and off at will?

'I don't know . . . She hasn't cried yet,' replied Adam.

'She's not one for crying is your mum. But she's feeling it. Give her some time, eh.'

Why didn't you give her some time, Adam thought. She cried for you. She felt it with you. Setting aside his food, Adam sighed. What his dad didn't know about him could fill a book. What he didn't see of him could be drawn on a giant canvas. And still he wouldn't understand.

'Anything else happen after the funeral?'

Adam snapped out of his reverie and turned to his dad.

'Like what?'

'Just, you know, anything?'

'No. Nothing,' replied Adam. *Not even tears.*

'Oh, OK. Did the solicitor not come around then?'

'Not that I know. Why would a solicitor come around?'

'Well, you know the old man worked for almost forty years for the underground. He must have a pension, and savings. That all needs to be sorted. You need a solicitor for that,' replied Adam's dad, taking a big bite and concentrating firmly on his burger.

'Mum hasn't said anything about it.'

'No, course not, probably doesn't want to worry you too much about that side of things. But you know, sooner it gets sorted, the better. Means a bit more cash, and you can stop working at that bloodbath, eh.' Adam's dad winked at him.

Something was niggling at Adam, but he couldn't quite pin it down. Something his dad wasn't saying . . .

'Anyway, forget that. I was thinking I could see Farah too one of these days. I don't think your mum's going to go for it, so I need your help. You need to be my inside man. Get me some face-time with the lady of the house.'

'She won't see you. You know that, Dad.'

'I know, but it's your birthday in a couple of days, right . . . ?'

Adam started. He'd completely forgotten about that.

'You see, I remembered this time. So if you say to her that you'd like it if I could come around for a bit of cake and tea, I get to see you and Farah too. We all win. But I need you onside.'

'I don't think she'll go for it, Dad. Not like that.'

A little flicker in his dad's eyes caught Adam's attention, making him tense. Glancing down, he saw fists turning into balls. Just as quickly, the anger passed and he felt a reassuring hand squeezing his shoulder.

'Come on, you have to try. We're a family and it's your sixteenth. You're well on the way to being a man. Look at you, almost as tall as me and everything!'

Adam squirmed and sat on his hands and looked straight ahead. William was gone, so was Dadda. This was the only father he had left. His dad was looking at him earnestly, bobbing his head. His eyes spoke of understanding and compassion, but those fists . . .

'OK, Dad. I'll try my best to make it happen.'

Beaming, Adam's dad put an arm around him and leaned back. Both father and son sat and watched as the pigeons swooped down in case there was some food on offer.

* * *

Laila looked across at Adam and sighed. He had barely said a word to her in the last two hours. His whole body had folded in on itself and the fire in his eyes, the embers she so enjoyed staring into, were ashes. If he would only open up to me, Laila thought. She had glanced at some of the drawings he'd been doing in his notepad and they were dark and ugly. All streaks and sharp scratches on the page. Nothing beautiful.

'Adam . . . ?'

'Huh?' Adam turned, snapping out of his thoughts.

'You with me?'

'Yeah, course.'

'I feel like you're walking alone somewhere on another planet, without me.'

Turning to her, Adam blinked and shook his head. 'I'm sorry.'

He sat up and took her hand in his. 'They're like dark clouds now – your eyes. Ripples of grey.'

'I'm not angry,' she said, squeezing his hand. 'I'm confused as to how I can help you.'

'Maybe you can't help me.'

'Is that what you think?' said Laila with a grimace.

'I'm just saying, some things can't be helped. You can't fix it for me. So, yeah, maybe you can't.'

Letting go of Adam's hand, Laila looked straight ahead, shaking her head.

'What?'

'You wanna deal with this by yourself?'

'I'm just saying, I don't know how it's all going to turn out. My life feels pretty messed up.'

'Do I feel pretty messed up?'

'No, no, that's not it. That's not what I'm saying.' *Tell her it's hard to explain. Tell her! Make her smile!*

'You're not saying anything, Adam! That's the problem! You want to be alone, fine. I get it! Be alone!'

Grabbing her bag, she held up her hands, as if this was a stick-up and Adam had pointed a gun at her.

'I have to go.'

Adam didn't move. Didn't say a word. As he watched her gradually become a point in the distance, Adam knew he was flying too close to the sun and this was what Icarus felt as he fell to earth.

Adam knew he had to find William. Somehow he knew William was what he and the Shah family needed. He had a heart in his body that belonged to them. He couldn't just leave like that. Adam didn't know how it was all supposed to work out, but he did know William needed to be with them.

In one of their conversations, William had mentioned the hostel he stayed in when he wasn't sleeping in Dadda's armchair. Hopping off the bus, Adam walked past the cinema and through the main square, running right into a group of protestors. One of the scribbled placards caught his eye. *Justice for Muslims! We are for peace!* A protester barged into him. This was the time now. Bombings, beheadings, kidnappings. Being born in 2001, Adam had never known a time when his people had not been in the news.

'Brother, come with us. Join the protest. Not all Muslims want to kill. Islam is a religion of peace. We need . . .'

Pushing past him, Adam nudged his way through the crowd. As ever, he didn't want to be part of a group. He wanted to be alone, apart. That was his way. Wasn't it? Emerging into a clear space, Adam turned to see a number of police cars parked on the main road. It looked like a peaceful protest, but maybe police were needed for crowd control. Some of the doors on the police vans slid open. Adam moved away off the main road towards the hostel. A bored-looking man at reception buzzed him in.

'Yep?' he asked, not looking up from the computer.

'Do you have a man called William Tide living here?'

'I can't tell you that, can I? It's confidential,' he replied, scowling.

'I need to get hold of him. It's very important,' said Adam, leaning over the counter and trying to catch the man's eye.

Sighing, the man looked Adam up and down.

'I can't just tell anyone who turns up and asks, understand? It don't work like that.' The man went back to looking at the screen.

'I'm related to him. He's part of our family.'

The man looked up at him, curious, and shook his head. 'Eh? You 'avin' a laugh. He's a pale bloke and you're . . . err . . . not. How's that work then?'

'So he does live here?'

Realising that he'd been tricked, the man stood up.

'Look, leave it out or I'll have to chuck you out.'

'Can I leave him a message?'

'Piss off,' the man replied, looking annoyed.

Adam backed away and walked out onto the street, happy that at least he knew where William was staying. He crossed the busy road and went looking for a sandwich to stave off the rumblings in his stomach. The market was busy, but he spotted at least seven police officers, trying not to look too conspicuous but failing miserably. It looked like something was about to kick off. A couple of older women had surrounded a young-looking officer and were asking him questions. Adam walked over and listened in on their conversation.

'What's going on, officer? Why the police vans?'

'Nothing to worry about, it's just a precaution. Just to keep the protest peaceful.'

'Five police vans to keep a few people with signs peaceful?'

'Look, it's just a precaution. Better safe than sorry.'

A few other voices chipped in then and the police officer began to look nervous.

'We heard there's a English Defence League group about to march down the hill. Is that true?' chipped in another man, and the small crowd began to swell.

The officer began to look nervous and held up his hands. 'Please, we have the situation under control. Let us deal with it.'

In less than a minute the news had gone from stall to stall. Taking that as a bad sign, a few stallholders began to pack up. Adam took a side street and crossed the road back to the main square. Standing back and watching the crowd, he wondered what it would feel like being part of the mob in front of him. All his life, every time he'd seen even a small group, he had made his excuses and left. Maybe the silence he favoured was because of the people around him. Farah, his mum, Dadda and then William. But there was more to it, something that always drew him to stand on the edge of the cliff beside Icarus, but unlike him, Adam was happy to stay grounded and stare at the sun. He tapped his temple with his index finger, trying to dislodge the thoughts in his head. Something caught his eye on the edge of the crowd, a familiar green coat. The swell of the crowd was rising and falling, filling his vision with a sea of colours. There it was again. Adam pushed his way forward, the flash of waxy green keeping just ahead of him. *Come on*, Adam thought, *come on, stop moving for just one second . . .*

Grabbing the coat, Adam yanked hard on the sleeve. William turned and registered that it was him.

'What are you doing here?'

'You can't just leave like that,' said Adam, still gripping William's sleeve. 'You belong with us.'

'Oh, Adam. I don't. Not really. You have been kind, but . . . only my heart does.'

Adam tried to pull William out of the ebb and flow of the growing crowd, which was beginning to jostle as the movement around them became choppy. It was becoming difficult not to be lifted off your feet as each ripple spread around them.

'Why are the police here?' asked Adam.

'Because of them,' replied William, pointing with his head in the direction of the hill.

Adam raised himself up on the balls of his feet to take a better look. A very different crowd was walking down the hill towards them. Adam caught glimpses of their banners. *England for the English. Islam = Terrorism. No More Mosques. No Surrender.*

Adam grabbed William's hand. 'Let's get out of here. This has nothing to do with us.'

'It feels like it has to do with all of—' William started saying, but without warning the movement of the crowd around them became erratic. There was a scream and then angry shouts. The police were locking shields and walking slowly towards the oncoming crowd. Objects were thrown, and a few people went down, clutching faces and heads. Adam saw broken bottles as little pockets of space began to open up. The other mob, the English Defence League, had now reached the police lines and were pushing against them, inching them back one step a time.

'William. You can't be here. You have to stay calm, protect your heart. Let's get out of here. Now.'

Practically dragging William, Adam pushed through the milling crowd as missiles rained down around them as they tried to get away. William was in a daze and shuffled after him. Flustered, Adam saw an alley and made for it. A police officer stood in their path.

'You can't come up here. Turn around and go back the other way.'

'We can't. It's blocked and this man has a heart condition. Please let us through. He only lives around the corner.'

'I can't. If I let you in, another ten will follow.'

'Please!' Adam pleaded. 'He can't have another heart attack. It's a new heart. A good heart, a working heart. Please.'

Making a sucking sound and taking a look at William, who was now visibly wilting, the policeman moved aside and ushered them past.

Propping William up was taking all his strength. Adam leaned against a wall.

'Let's go somewhere quiet. Follow me, we'll go visit the old man,' he said, and pulled William away from the crowds towards the cemetery.

The wind buffeted them as they walked down the narrow paths in the graveyard. William still looked pale and pinched and, walking slowly, took in large gulps of air every few steps. They walked in silence past the neat rows. Everything was so ordered. Graves planted in a grid, each plot a point on a piece of graph paper, each grave allocated a number and each person a set distance from the next. Adam thought how a lot of people died in pain or agony or with regret or sadness, but that once you were dead all that was redundant, and all that was left was this: the map of the dead. He led William through the first part of the graveyard, which William called 'the people of the cross'. As they walked ahead in silence, gradually the crosses began to merge into half-moons and they were close. Treading with care, Adam made his way to his Dadda's grave. William had stopped at a bench and sat down, watching him. Feeling awkward standing up, Adam knelt down next to the grave. He wanted to speak, wanted to say something, wanted to speak with his Dadda like he never had in life. But the words wouldn't come. Adam started clearing the grave of twigs and rocks, smoothing the soil until it was flat. A clear canvas. With a twig Adam scrawled into the mud.

Hearttoheart. Hearttwoheart.
Twohearts. Too hurt hearts.

Adam sat there a while, hoping real words would come to him or tears even, but none did. He heard William behind him. William stood over the grave, stared at the words Adam had scraped into the mud and started speaking.

'I don't know why you did it. I don't know why I was the one to get your heart. I don't know about any of it. I do know that you have a good family. Good people that have been good to me. I want you to know that at least. I know you're there in that grave with a big hole in your chest. A big chasm where your heart should be. A hole deep and wide and full of things you wanted to say to your family. So I'm trying to be useful to them. I'm going to try to watch over them. I don't understand all of it, and there are a few things still out of my reach, but I know that I'll get there. I'm no good with words. That's what I used to say to me mam, and she'd say, "I wasn't too good with actions either." She was all the family I ever had and she let me live but not love. This is love. Where I am now, with your family. The love owed you is now given to me. I didn't want to come here today, but now that I'm here I want you to know that I'm grateful. As selfish as it sounds, I'm glad you gave me your heart, because that has allowed me to love. For the first time in my life, it has allowed me to be a part of something.'

William stopped speaking.

'You know what?' said Adam, after a pause. 'Most people leave behind money, houses, family heirlooms, letters and all that kind of stuff.'

'Yeah, they do.'

'But my Dadda left behind his heart. I would have just been happy with a watch or something, you know.'

'Yeah, I know, but I'm quite attached to mine,' replied William and began to laugh.

Adam began to laugh too. The wind continued to whistle round them, whipping the leaves about the two figures, carrying their laughter across the rows of the dead and beyond to the land of the living.

'Let's play a word game, William. We use the word heart in so many ways. First one to drop one, buys fish and chips. Ready? I'll start . . . Heartbeat . . .'

William: Heart attack
Adam: Heartless
W: Heart sore
A: Heartbroken
W: Cold heart
A: Braveheart
W: Great heart
A: Sweetheart
W: Half-hearted
A: Heart of stone
W: Heart of gold
A: Pure of heart
W: Kind hearted
A: Lionheart

W: Take heart

A: Hard-hearted

W: Stony-hearted

A: Light-hearted

W: Faint-hearted

A: Chicken-hearted

W: Heart-shaped

A: Heart of the matter

W: Heavy heart

A: Heart-warming

W: Heartful

A: Heartache

W: Big-hearted

A: Soft-hearted

W: Dis-heartened

A: Open heart

W: Blackheart

A: Erm . . . Erm . . . Aaargh! I give up.

W: I have one more . . .

A: Show-off.

W: Heartsick

A: Nice. End on a positive note.

W: Yeah, thanks. I'll have a haddock, please.

The doors to the operating theatre were closed as Adam peered through the square-cut windows. He was back in the hospital, but this time not in the green patient's gown. Looking at his hands, Adam again saw that they weren't his. They were delicate, like his, but different. Something covered his mouth, a tight elasticated cap on his head stretched over his scalp.

'Glad you'll be assisting on this one,' said Mr Desai.

'Me too.' That wasn't his voice. What was happening?

Adam felt himself move towards the sinks. He felt hot water and soap being rubbed into his hands. Hands that were not his hands. He didn't want to look behind him. Not yet. He knew that lying there on the operating table, connected to wires and tubes, was his Dadda. Slowly and with purpose, the body that was not his moved towards the operating table where another doctor and two nurses were waiting. His Dadda was attached to oxygen, but his eyes were glazed. One foot in this world and the other jamming the door to the next.

The first cut was to divide the breastbone, opening the chest cavity and clamping the ends in place. Adam's eyes widened as the heart was slowly revealed. Confused, disoriented, he tried to make sense of what was in front of him by closing his eyes. He imagined the peeled-back skin as a flower that had opened, the first of the season, containing a prize within. He imagined a bee picking up its scent from a distance and angling towards it. A honeysuckle heart. A heart that gave sustenance. A heart that gave life. That was what was in his mind's eye. An open heart. Still beating as he snipped away the delicate threads holding it in place. Adam stared at his Dadda in fascination and horror as the surgeon, with watchmaker's patience, continued to sever links between the heart and the body. Each cut made Adam flinch, each tug made Adam blink. It was easy to lift the heart out from his Dadda's chest, tiny tendrils still attached to it, and for the first time Adam saw a heart as it was. *Your heart is the size of your clenched fist.* And it was. A bloody fist. He saw himself remove the heart, a slab of meat no different to those at the butcher's, and place it in a cool box. And that was it, his Dadda was gone. Kept alive long enough to give life, but now it was more about the living. The operating theatre emptied, following the living heart out of the room and into the next. Turning his head, Adam saw a carcass sprawled on the operating table, clamps still in place, wires and pipes sprouting from his chest like weeds, but what caught Adam's eye was a flash of green. His last view as he left the room was his Dadda's hand that was hanging limp over the edge of the operating table, a green opal ring on his left index finger.

He saw himself discard the bloody gloves and gown and felt the hot water washing over his hands again. William lay on the table in the next theatre, chest open to the world, ready to receive another chance at life. He had already been prepped and was sedated and unaware of what was happening to him. But do you know what just happened to my Dadda? Do you know that he's lying in the next room discarded, clamped open, arm dangling? Adam took his place beside William and watched as the surgeon produced his Dadda's heart from the cool box. Adam had expected a delicate lowering, a surgically precise implant, but the heart was placed into the shallow grave of a hole and then the work began. He saw the surgeon's hands work quickly, not wasting a single movement, attaching, incising, suturing, knotting and sealing all the valves of the heart. Blood flowed into the heart cavity and was quickly vacuumed by a pump, but the crimson liquid was hungry. Adam imagined the clamps to be dams; once raised the blood would thunder into the heart valves. But something was wrong. Streams of blood had already flowed over the heart, but it was yet to start beating. Adam looked up at the other surgeon, who nodded.

'We're going to have to jolt it.'

'OK.'

Adam looked down at his hands. Not a tremor or a shake affected them. A nurse handed him two small paddles which he attached. They stood back and an electrical surge was pulsed into the heart, involuntarily jerking William's body. Still nothing. The heart sat in its new shell, unmoved.

'Again, please,' he heard himself saying.

Another pulse pricked the heart and Adam looked up to see William's eyes flicker open for a second. *William, it's me,* Adam screamed, their eyes meeting, a flicker of recognition before William lapsed out of life once more. Adam stared at the heart. *Beat! Please beat!* Blood flowed into the heart cavity and with a twitch the heart flickered to life. *There!* A subtle contracting as the blood, deprived by the vacuum, flooded the cavity and the heart began to pulse. Slowly at first, ventricle and aorta stretching in their new surroundings for the first time until the heart filled the space. The beat quickened and now the heart was pulsating at a vibrant pace, fist squeezing, urgent and new and alive. Holding up his bloody hands, Adam nodded at the surgeon opposite him. He began to carefully suture the remaining connections, checking all five strands to make sure everything was attached and complete. Unlike his Dadda, who was incomplete. Who would be stitched up and buried without a heart. They removed the clamps and the skin was stretched back over the breastbone. Deftly, Adam used wires to close the cavity before he could begin the final stitching. Finally he tied a knot, pulling the threads tightly across the chest, before cutting off the excess suture thread and sealing the chest. Adam turned to look at William, who was still drifting, eyes half closed. Suddenly, William's eyes flickered open, bloodshot and wild. Sitting up, he looked down at his chest, at the brutal stitching, and turned to Adam. Reaching towards him, he tugged at the wires, the stitches pulling taut against his skin.

'What have you done?' he said, grabbing Adam's hand. 'What have you done?!'

Adam woke to William shaking him gently. Adam sucked in large gulps of air and stared at William.

'You were talking in your sleep,' said William. Adam blinked his eyes and shook his head, trying to clear it.

'It was a dream. So real. I was there.'

'Where?'

'In the operating theatre with Dadda, then I . . . I saw the heart removed from him then put into you. I saw everything. I felt everything.'

William nodded and sighed. Hooking his right hand over his left shoulder, he stood up.

'You were talking for a long time in your sleep. I didn't want to shake you . . .'

'I was the surgeon in the dream, William. I made the cuts. I stitched you up. I've never had a dream like that before.' Holding up his hands Adam saw that they were shaking. Not like a surgeon's hands. Closing his fists, he squeezed his hands, imitating the beating of a heart. Two fists, two hearts. So many stitches and cuts and repaired tissue and marrow and blood. So much blood.

William looked up at the frowning grey clouds. The sky was angry, and he knew that meant any minute now hot tears would fall. Going for a walk had been Adam's idea. After insisting on meeting William's doctor, he would accompany him on a daily walk that would improve his lung capacity and help his breathing. William liked the walks and the quiet conversations they had.

'It's going to pour down,' said Adam, looking up at the sky.

'Yeah, we'd better get home,' replied William. Chuckling to himself, he shook his head. *Home*. Home to Farah and Yasmin and Daddima.

'Keep laughing to yourself like that, William, people gonna think you're crazy,' said Adam, but he was smiling. He enjoyed these walks too, the quiet, solid presence of William comforted him, their conversations about ideas and people giving him somewhere to park his thoughts.

William turned to see Adam looking up at something.

'What's up?' asked William, walking back to where Adam was standing.

'It's a church,' replied Adam, pointing to the sign.

'Yeah, and?'

'Do all churches have confession? I've only seen it in films. Is that where you speak to a priest and tell him all the bad things you've done?' asked Adam.

'I haven't been for years. Dad was a Catholic and used to make Mum go to church with him, and she just carried on going after he'd left and used to drag me with her. Confession is a way of getting things off your chest. Things you feel bad about.'

Adam thought about it and realised there wasn't anything similar at the local mosque. You could talk to the imam there but it wasn't quite the same.

'It sounds like it could be useful.'

'It could be, I suppose, if you have something you need to confess,' replied William.

Adam nudged him.

'Did you realise why I stopped at this church?'

'No?' replied William.

'The name. Of the church. Did you see it?'

William looked up at the blue sign with gold lettering. *Church of the Sacred Heart.*

'We're in the right place then,' said William with a smile, and followed Adam through the door. 'OK, I can see someone's in there right now so just wait here. You remember what you have to say?'

'Yep. I got it.'

'Look, someone's just left and the priest's taking a break. Go on.'

Adam slid the door open and, closing it behind him, sat down. Feeling nervous, he took out his notepad and pencil to calm himself. He thought of the image he'd seen illuminated on the stained-glass window as he'd walked in. Of dawn and the sun rising.

Daybreak. Daybroke, Daybroken, Broken Days.

Hearing a shuffling in the other half of the booth and the screen being pulled back, Adam hurried to put his pad and pencil away and sat up straight. He wasn't quite sure why, but he felt that was appropriate.

'Bless me, Father, for I have sinned,' said Adam in a firm voice.

'Go on, my son . . .'

'This is my first confession!' Adam blurted out.

'It's never too late to confess, my son. If you are penitent, God will hear you and forgive. Go on . . .'

'I don't know where to begin . . .'

'You are safe here. Go on, my son. Confess and lay the burden down.'

'I've lied to my little sister. Just to make her go away.'

'Go on . . .'

'I've argued with my mum, even when I've known I was wrong, because I was angry at her. I've tried to make her cry, but it was for her own good.'

'Go on, my son . . .'

'There was this time I took a pound from my grandmother's purse. I was short for some spray cans.'

'Yes . . .'

'Is this the right type of confession stuff . . . ?' asked Adam, a little flustered.

'There is no right or wrong type of confession, my child. Go on,' replied the priest.

'I am ashamed of myself about one thing in particular. Of standing there and doing nothing. Of running away and covering my ears when I was younger. My father . . . he used to hit my mother and she would stand there and take it. She would sob to herself quietly and take it. I would be in the other room, and I didn't do anything to stop it . . . I mean, he would hit me too, but that was OK, I could live with it, but I should have done something . . .'

'You were a child. It was not for you to do something,' replied the priest.

'Yeah, but once the neighbours or somebody called the police. When they knocked on the door, my dad went out to meet them and took me along. That was my chance, you see . . . They asked me if everything was OK. If there was a problem. I could have told them everything, I could have, but I chose not to. Because he's my dad and I didn't want him to go away from us or get into trouble. But everything was not OK.'

There was silence on the other side and some shuffling.

'My child, what you did was not a sin. You were afraid and you did what you thought was right. That's not a sin. It's not your fault you didn't speak, but you're speaking to me now and that's a good step.'

'But if I had done something then, it wouldn't have got as far as it did. It wouldn't have got to more fists and violence and I wouldn't have left that door open . . .'

'What door, my child?'

'I left the door open and she fell. Like Icarus, she fell and now she doesn't speak.'

'What door? Who fell, my child? Who doesn't speak?'

Adam opened the door and ran from the booth, sprinting past William without stopping.

The priest came up behind William, looking troubled.

'I wasn't able to absolve that child of his sins.'

'The sins are not his, Father,' replied William, moving to follow Adam out of the large double doors.

William found Adam sitting on a bench in the street nearby, elbows resting on his knees, head low.

'What happened? What did you confess?'

'I didn't. I couldn't tell him,' replied Adam without looking up.

'Tell him what?'

'About Farah. Why she doesn't talk. About what happened to her. Because I left a door open.'

'Tell me . . .'

'I can't. I *can't*. I should've been looking after her, I should've . . .'

'Tell me,' urged William.

Adam looked up, his mind reliving the moments, and finally began to speak.

We were drawing and messing about in the living room. Like we always did. I was scribbling in my pad, watching Farah as she tried to copy me. She held the pencil in her chubby fingers and made large circles. Stopping to see if I was watching her after every scribble. I gave her the thumbs up each time, making her squeal and encouraging her to try again. I finished my sketch and showed her a drawing of a figure with wings, hands outstretched, and she smiled, pointing at it. The door to the living room was closed, but we could still hear Mum and Dad arguing. Again. We tried to ignore them and carried on, but the sound carried through the door, filling the empty spaces in the living room. Farah's ears pricked up, a frown creeping onto her face. I flicked through my notepad and showed her another drawing, trying to distract her. But there were other sounds now. Sounds we both recognised. Sobbing. Hard sounds. I got up and went to stand by the door. We could hear things being thrown. Farah stood unsteady on her little legs and tottered to stand by my side, grabbing my hand. I smiled, trying to calm her. As young as she

was, Farah knew it wasn't a real smile. Leading her back to the notepad, I sat her down and put the pencil back in her hand. Eventually she set about scribbling in her book once again. I went back to the door and signalled to her, Shhh. I'll be back in a minute. Draw something nice for me.

Pulling the door open, I slipped out. Another crash. In my hurry I forgot to pull the door closed behind me. The angry sounds. The crashing sounds. The sobbing sounds. Sounds I had heard for years now as I took each step. Each step was a reminder of how this house had never known peace. Each step took me closer to the eye of the storm. At the top of the stairs I stopped and waited. What would I do? What could I do? I knew the answer to that. What I had done in the past. Get in the way. Be a distraction. Take the hurt onto myself. I knew by now how that could be done. The sounds continued, coming from the bedroom. I knocked on the door and took a step back.

'Leave her alone,' I said, making sure my voice would carry.

'Adam, please go downstairs. It's OK, just go down,' came my mum's voice, wavering and unsteady.

'No. I won't. Stop fighting – you're scaring Farah.'

'Please, Adam . . .' said Mum.

Another crash, swearing, and things being kicked over.

Just as I was about to go into the bedroom, the door opened and my dad appeared.

Light flooding from behind him, he stood, a silhouette in the doorway. I saw Mum, her face bloody, hair pulled in all directions, body bent over on the floor in pain.

'What do you want?'

'Leave her alone.'

'You want to give me some lip, boy? Do you?'

'Don't hit her.'

'Who should I hit then? You?'

'Yeah, hit me.'

Scowling, he turned away and made to close the door. Jamming my foot in the door, I shook my head.

'Leave her alone.'

Grabbing my T-shirt, my father lifted me from my feet and dragged me across the landing. Mum screamed and stood up, clutching her stomach.

'I told you to go away, boy. You're just like her. You don't listen. And people who don't listen end up getting hurt.'

'We're not people. We're your family.'

'Well, if you listened, I might treat you like family.'

Flinging me to the ground, Dad stood over me. Grabbing his leg, I shook my head once more.

'Leave her alone.'

'I warned you, boy . . .' said Dad.

I don't remember if Dad was using fists or palms or feet. I didn't know if he was kicking me or punching me. In these moments, I usually found a sense of calm. A place I could go that wasn't here. Was elsewhere. As each blow connected with my body, I absorbed it. Took it into myself and sent it elsewhere. I knew I was probably grunting in pain, screaming even, but I couldn't hear it. After a while I felt softer hands, cradling my head. A smell I knew. Of lemons and chopped coriander. Mum held me close, as the blows still rained down. A downpour. Something made me come back to myself. Standing at the top of the stairs on unsteady legs was Farah. Eyes wide with shock, she stood pointing at Dad. Mum made a small crumpled sound, but I wasn't listening. Dad hadn't spotted Farah, and grabbing Mum's hair dragged her across the carpet towards the stairs. I scrambled, trying to untangle hurt limbs.

'No, Dad, no. Behind you!'

Dragging Mum by the hair, Dad swung his free hand to strike her again, and clipped Farah on the head. Farah reached out for me, holding her hands out, stretching every sinew and fingertip, but she was already falling. And just like that, the anger in the house evaporated. Dad fell to his knees as Mum rushed down the stairs to Farah who lay at the bottom. She looked peaceful to me. Serene. Almost as if she was having a nap. Mum stroked her hair, spoke her name, afraid to move her. Each step groaned as I raced down, punctuating the low keening from Mum. Kneeling beside Farah, I held her hand, squeezing it. Eyes flashing open, she looked right at me. She opened her mouth, but no sound came. She tried again, but there was nothing. Mum gathered her in and held her close to her chest. Resting her head on Mum's shoulder, Farah looked at me. There were no words.

Adam looked for Laila daily, but she was avoiding him. Seeing Cans leaning against a wall bobbing his head, Adam waved and made his way over.

'Wassup?' said Cans, pulling Adam in for an embrace.

'Same ol shit,' replied Adam. 'What you listening to?'

Cans's face lit up.

'Serious, I made a mixtape with some pro tools software. Man, you don't know about that software – it's a miracle maker.'

'Let me hear. What did you remix?' asked Adam, smiling.

Cans pulled off his headphones and popped them on Adam's head.

'Sounds good,' said Adam after a while, handing the headphones back.

'Good? *Good?* That's all you can say, you with all those scribbled words . . . Aargh.'

'Have to listen to the original again, but sounds like you've stripped it down and made it more, err . . . basic?'

'Exactly. Stripped it down to its basic. Essential elements only, you get me.'

Adam did. He understood what Cans had done, stripping away layers of sounds, almost working in reverse so that the song was in the early stages of production. Sometimes Adam would do that with his own drawings and paintings. Would strip the layers off until he was back to the first few scribbles and strokes. At the point when anything was still possible. Looking at Cans as he listened again, right hand signing the beat, head twitching, Adam wished he could strip some of the layers of his own life and reset it back to when there were still different possibilities. He wished there was some editing software with advanced tools for his life.

Cans glanced at him and took off his headphones.

'You've got that faraway look again. Come back these ends, fam.'

'I'm here, I'm here,' replied Adam, trying to focus.

'What you been up to recently? How's the heart dude?'

'He's all right. You know, keeping it together, under the circumstances.'

'And you?' asked Cans.

'I dunno, bruv. Life feels mad-crazy at the moment. I told you bout it last time, it's a lot, you get me?'

'From what you told me last time, it's mad-crazy-beautiful, bruv. If your life was a track I was mixing, I'd try to add some mellow into the mix, man. Just to keep you settled, you know.'

'Tell you what, why don't you mix one for me? A song for Adam.'

'You're on. Probably some acoustic number, so you could stare off into the distance all deep an that.'

'Yeah, whatever.'

'No, come on, I'll do one for you. A special Cans remix.'

'You seen her about?'

'Eh? Seen who?' Cans pretended to fiddle with his headphone wire. Adam glared until he looked up at him.

'Oh, *her*. Erm, a few times in passing . . .'

'When? Recently?'

'The other day . . . Look, fam, maybe you wanna call that one . . .'

'Why do you say that?' asked Adam, agitated.

'I'm just sayin, maybe she's not for you, bruv,' replied Cans, looking at his feet.

'What you sayin?'

'Look, I saw her the other day, yesterday. She was with that dude, you know him.'

Adam's chest tightened and he gritted his teeth.

'Who?'

'That tall one that hangs around with all those wasteman.'

'Faze?' asked Adam in a hoarse voice.

'Yeah, him. Tall boy.'

Leaning against the wall, Adam turned away from Cans and looked straight ahead. He'd been so stupid, pushing her away. Not sharing his stuff with her. He'd told her just a bit and then clammed up. And now she was no longer with him.

'Come on, bruv, it don't matter. You're the better man. You've just got things going on in your life. She must know that, so it's her choice. If she can't help you now, she can't help you. You get me?'

Looking up at Cans, he nodded. She did know about him. She knew it was difficult right now, so why would she disappear like that? And with Faze too?

'Come on, bruv, the bell's about to go. Let's get to our lesson and forget about her . . .'

Adam walked along with Cans in a daze. He didn't want to be here. The buzzing static of everybody around him was driving him insane.

'I've got to go. I can't be here.'

'What? Where you got to be?'

'I have a place. Wanna come?'

Cans looked at his watch and grimaced.

'Yeah, go on then. It's only our final year and the rest of our lives and all that.'

As they trudged away from the school, Adam tried to empty his head of Laila, but all he could think about was her storm-filled eyes.

Cans whistled low and long as they stood looking out over the dead trains. Adam watched his expression change as he grasped what Adam was trying to do.

'How long you been at this now?' asked Cans, awe in his voice.

'About a month, almost every night,' replied Adam, surprised himself at how hard he'd worked on it.

'It's crazy. You're one crazy guy.' Cans shook his head. 'It's sick.'

Adam smiled, and for the first time in a long time relaxed and looked over his work. It had been hard going at times, especially in the cold, bending low over the freezing metal, struggling not to get paint on his clothes and keeping to his original plan. Cans looked at him with different eyes and continued to shake his head at him.

'It's epic, man. This is some historically epic shit right here.'

'Yo, I was aiming for epic,' replied Adam, beaming.

'Trust you not to be satisfied with just painting on a canvas or a wall like everyone else. You have to be extra, still.'

'It's been somewhere I could get away from my other self. Sometimes even get away from my head. When I'm up here in the dark, it feels like I'm painting on top of the world, and only God's watching.'

Cans looked at Adam curiously and whistled again. Turning on his heels, he spun around, almost toppling off the train. Righting himself, he pointed at Adam.

'Whatever else is happening, man, you're in control of this, your art. Only you in your whole life, no matter what happens, you will always have this. Pick up a pencil or a brush or a spray can and that's it.'

Adam looked over the trains and shook his head. 'Nothing lasts forever. Nothing stays the same. I don't know why I did it.'

'Does it need a reason?'

'Nah, I suppose it doesn't.'

'I think that's how it's supposed to be, bruv.'

Adam looked at his work and nodded.

'Just, don't sign this one, my G. It's gonna have to be one of those anonymous works. But we'll both know where the legend began,' said Cans, thumping his chest.

'My brother. Yeah, we'll know, and that's all that matters.'

'Why did you agree to this, William?'

'I didn't agree to it. Your mum told me I had to do it!'

Adam glanced at William and pursed his lips, pretending to be annoyed, but really he was happy William was there. Ever since he had started school, Adam had hated parents' evenings. He hated the teachers dismantling his character bit by bit until all he was left with was *must try harder*. He hated that they all said he was *a bit of a dreamer* and didn't *join in* with the others. He hated that they picked up on his inability to listen, follow instructions or complete the work. Adam was glad his mum wasn't coming. That was a lot of hate for her to handle.

'OK, here's the deal. Most of the teachers will say that I've got no chance at getting through. That I don't listen, that I don't work hard enough and that I'm just not cut out for college.'

'And would that be true?' asked William.

'No, not really . . .'

'What do you mean, not really?'

'Well, they all seem to think I'm some kind of empty shell of a boy with no idea of what's going on.'

'But you're not,' said William.

'No, I might be an empty shell of a boy, but I do know what's going on.'

'Smart-arse. Bet a few of them say that too,' replied William.

'Probably. Look, this school, the teachers are under fire. They just haven't got time to always teach. Most of the time it's just crowd control.'

'Yeah, but you could still help yourself. You're not one of those kids who hasn't got it.'

'I don't know what sort of kid I am, William. I can draw – that's about it.'

'Well, that's a start. Let's see what they have to say.' William walked ahead of Adam into the school hall.

As William and Adam made their way to the first appointment, a few people began to turn towards them and stare. Some nodded at Adam, but most turned to look at William as he eased past them to wait patiently in a queue.

'They're all looking at us,' said William under his breath.

'A tall *pale* dude and a skinny *brown* kid walk into a crowded hall . . .'

'Smart-arse,' said William.

'It could be a good joke though,' mused Adam. 'A friend of mine told me I was too serious, so I'm trying to be more light-hearted.'

William nodded and took a look around the room. Different areas had been allocated according to subject. Humanities in one corner, sciences in the other. Art in the middle, PE near the door.

'Who's first?' asked William.

'Maths. Mrs Green.'

Straightening up, William held out his hand and smiled.

'Hello, Mrs Green, I'm William.'

Mrs Green looked at Adam and raised a slim eyebrow. Always calculating, thought Adam. He would have to share that one with William later.

'He's with me. My mum couldn't make it – she had to work. Here's a note.' Producing a crumpled piece of paper, Adam handed it to the teacher and sat down.

Passing the note back to Adam, Mrs Green smiled at William. 'Good to meet you, Mr Tide. I'm glad somebody could make it this time. You didn't get here at all last time, did you, Adam?'

'No, miss,' replied Adam, folding and refolding the piece of paper.

'Well, I have to say, I'm very concerned about Adam. The exams are only a few months away and, to be totally honest, I don't really know if he's going to make it. I have had some occasional pieces of homework from him, but I couldn't tell you what level he's working at. He's a mystery to me.'

William looked at the maths teacher and nodded. Adam had told him to nod every few seconds and say 'sure', 'of course', and 'I understand' whenever possible. He explained that teachers liked that.

'I understand,' tried William.

'Do you? I wish I did,' spluttered Mrs Green, looking at Adam.

Looking sideways at Adam, William wondered what it would be best to say now. Concentrating on smoothing out his note, Adam shrugged his shoulders. William looked the teacher in the eye.

'Can he do the work?' asked William.

'Well, I think he can. I might know more if he did more regular work for me.'

Each teacher had their say: Adam was good at all sports. Except he often forgot to get involved in the game. He liked standing on the periphery watching. Adam wasn't interested in experiments. But he did like the technical drawings of insects, especially moths. That wouldn't get him a C grade though.

His geography teacher, Mr Mackintosh, said Adam had a very good sense of place. He only wished he would find this place and hand in his coursework.

For history, Mrs Faulkner said Adam's grasp of great events from the past was good. The hope was that he would drag this knowledge into the present and do some work for her. His English teacher, Mr Gray, said Adam was a keen student of literature, his understanding of texts sophisticated and measured. That he wrote well – that he had a startling imagination. But he won't pass his exams. He doesn't write how the exam boards want. It was a shame, he said, because he rather liked how Adam wrote.

William nodded and smiled and listened carefully. This was the first time he'd been in a school in over thirty-five years. Each teacher said similar things but in different ways. But it was the look in their eyes that did it for William. A look that said, no, he wasn't always present, and no, he didn't always do the work. But he could. As the evening went on, Adam became more fidgety, but William smiled at him. After each appointment, he patted him on the back. Adam was confused. Each teacher was less complimentary than the last and every teacher said he was likely to fail. So why was William smiling?

'Who's next?'

'She's not here yet. We have to wait. It's not been good so far,' said Adam, looking sidelong at William.

'I think it's been good.'

Adam stared at William.

'Were you listening to them?'

'Yeah. They all said that you can do the work.'

'That's not what they said. They said I never did any work.'

'That's different from not being able to do the work.'

'Is it?'

Now William looked sidelong at Adam.

'Yeah.'

'Mum would be laying into me about now.'

'You can do the work. That's better than not being able to do it at all,' said William.

'When did you become Mr Glass Half Full?'

'About the time you became Mr Half Empty,' replied William.

Adam muttered something under his breath, but was glad William was there. Something had changed in him over the past few months since he'd come to them, and the whole family had benefited from his solid presence.

'My last teacher might actually say something good about me.'

'Best for last, eh?'

'Something like that,' replied Adam, as he led William towards Miss Matheson. She sat as she usually did, looking at some picture in a large heavy book. Adam was sure he recognised it. It was one of his favourites.

'Is that the book with Icarus in it, miss?'

'Yes, it is,' replied Mrs Matheson, looking up and fixing them with a welcoming smile. 'Would you like to see it?'

Adam nodded as William sat down and leaned in close.

'Do you know the myth of Icarus, Mr . . . ?'

'Tide. Yes, but only because of Adam. He has sketches of Icarus in his notebook.'

'Yes, it's a favourite myth of his. Has he told you that he's going to use Icarus as the basis of his final piece in the exam?'

'No. No, he hasn't.'

Adam looked at his hands, long tapered fingers flickering, flexing.

'Yes, it's very exciting. You know, it's a joy to have Adam in my class. There's nothing he can't draw, but that's not why I like his work. It's that he draws it as he sees it and not necessarily as it should be. Does that make sense?'

'No, but that sounds like Adam,' replied William.

'OK, let me try to explain. Most of my students will represent on the page what they see with little or no interpretation of their own. A lot of them are very good at drawing, better even than Adam, but their work has nothing of themselves in it. With Adam, he's on the page. He's in every scribble and scratch of his pencil. He questions in every drawing what art is. And each time he breaks his image down to its true essence. Does that make any sense?'

Looking from Mrs Matheson to Adam, William nodded. 'No.'

'Good,' she replied, beaming. 'That's how it should be. I love his work and I think his ability to break down and rebuild his work time and time again will see him become a true artist. But. Exams don't work like that. They have structures and forms. Adam doesn't like working to those constraints. He pointedly ignores them. As good as his work is, he might not pass the art exam.'

William put his hand on Adam's shoulder and nodded. 'He sees the world in a unique way. His drawings astound me. I think it's important he draws the way he sees the world. Come what may.'

The little creases around Mrs Matheson's eyes deepened and she laughed. 'Well, yes, exactly! His talent will out no matter what, but I do wish he could make it to art school or something similar. He would do well.'

'He'll always be making art, it's in his nature, but the reality is that his mum needs help with the house. There isn't enough money. There's never enough. Art takes a back seat.'

'I understand, but I'll be keeping an eye on Adam. We're going to make sure his talent isn't wasted.'

'Thank you,' said William offering his right hand and covering Miss Matheson's hand with his left.

He felt a tug on his shirt and turned to Adam.

'Adam has something to give you,' said William, smiling at Adam's shyness.

'Don't wanna embarrass you, miss. It's a drawing,' said Adam, and quickly followed William out and away.

Mrs Matheson looked at the torn-off piece of paper and smiled, the deep furrows near her eyes creasing in pleasure as with great care she slipped the paper into her favourite book, pressing it closed.

William reflected on the evening as he walked with Adam though the quiet back streets. He realised that accompanying Adam to his parent–teacher evening was the first thing he'd done in a very long time that mattered, that made him feel that he was more than just a little cog, feel as if he was the wheel at the centre of the movement. He looked across at Adam as he trudged alongside him, hood up, head down, shoulders drooped. William knew Adam carried such a weight. Of violence and of loss. He wanted to reach out to him, and say the right words in the right order so that everything would be right again.

'You know, they all said the way you're going, you've got no chance . . .'

Adam smiled but his face was wearing a grim expression. 'I told you they would say that.'

'But I don't believe it,' replied William firmly.

'What's the point though, William? However hard you try – people still die, get sick, leave, hurt you or let you down. So I can sketch a bit. So what? My dad walked out on us, my mum can barely look at me without seeing him, my sister can't speak, my Dadda lived in his own head and then died, and then there's you. I mean, what's anybody supposed to do with that?'

William looked away, deflated, buffeted by Adam's anguish. Adam saw his stricken face.

'I didn't mean it like that. I was just saying . . .'

'It's OK, I understand, I get it.'

Adam hunched his shoulders.

'It's not you, I just feel all over the place. I can't explain it, but I could probably draw it for you . . .'

'I'd like that, Adam, I really wou—'

'Oi!'

Adam heard a shout behind him and turned to see a group of boys approaching. They had their hoods up, but Adam recognised the tallest figure as Faze.

'All right,' said Faze, nodding.

One of the other boys pointed at William and sniggered. 'This the paedo?' he said, and the group broke out into short, sharp snorts of laughter.

Faze stood to the side, hands in his pockets. Adam looked at Faze and then at each boy in turn. He signalled with his head to William and made to leave.

'Oi! Where you going, paedo? We heard you've got a nasty scar on your chest. We want to see it. Gis a look.'

Adam turned then, his anger rising to the surface. Felt his frustration grinding his teeth, his heartbeat quicken.

'Why don't you just fuck off? His scar's got nothing to do with you.'

The boy said something to his mates to make them laugh again, then turned suddenly and pushed Adam, making him stumble. Faze looked as if he would intervene, but hung back even so, hood covering his face.

'Got a big mouth for a paedo-lover, haven't ya? Let's have a look. You been knifed, innit? We just wanna look,' the boy said, taking a step towards William, who stood stock still, panicked. Adam moved in front of William and pushed the boy back into his friends, who grabbed Adam and pulled him away. The remaining boy moved towards William, who was breathing heavily now and sweating.

'What's wrong with you? Why you all sweaty for? Let's take a look,' he said, grabbing at William's shirt.

William could only feebly swat the boy's hand away as he struggled to breathe, but that did little to stop him coming on. Adam shouted and fought but he was now pinned down. Faze had still not moved and was now looking at his feet. The boy yanked hard at William's shirt. The sound of material ripping and buttons popping made Adam stop struggling as a patch of shirt came away in the boy's hand. In front of them all stood William with his shirt hanging in tatters. There was silence as they all stared at the scar running down William's chest. It was purple and raised, the skin angry at the memory of the scalpel and hands that had opened it. The boys stared in disbelief at the brutal scar, the shock freezing them in place.

Adam pulled free of the other boys and stood up. The anger had subsided and all that remained were shock and embarrassment. Faze was the first to move. Grabbing the boy who had ripped William's shirt, he shoved him away from William.

'Let's go,' he said to the others without looking back.

Adam watched them go, deflated as all the nervous energy left his body.

William had made no move to cover up.

'They tell you that they're going to open you up,' William said. 'But you never expect that means slicing you in half.'

194

'It looks so vicious,' replied Adam, unable to tear his eyes from William's chest.

'At least this scar is visible and it'll heal,' replied William, zipping up his jacket.

Adam pulled down his hood and stared at William. 'Earlier, when I was talking, I didn't mean you were the problem. You've helped us, made us heal a little. It's just that there's a lot going on,' he said.

'I know that. This is all new to me too. Living and caring. I didn't do too much of those before.'

Adam slipped in beside William and, using his arm to support William's elbow, he walked with him along the dark streets, each retreating into the silent land of their thoughts as the mist formed around them.

Adam slapped the mop onto the floor. The sloshing and swirling made a satisfying sound. After half an hour, he stood back and looked at his work. The floor was definitely cleaner, but no amount of scrubbing could erase some of the bloody marks. He looked around the empty shop. His ears picked up the constant hum of the freezers and the strip lighting, reminding him of something. Then a rap on the front door startled him and dislodged the thought from his head. William was standing outside peering in. Adam ushered him in and quickly shut the door behind him.

'You all right?' he asked, looking William up and down.

'Yeah. You?' replied William, doing the same.

Since the attack by the boys in the street, another shared trauma, they had become close. Adam thought of all that bound them now. Sadness, grief, pain, violence. These things had brought William to them. Strangely, an image of his maths teacher popped into his head.

'You know, Adam, everything has a formula. Even abstract things like love. The formula is the combination that unlocks the safe. Sometimes the wheel is turned forward, sometimes backwards, sometimes it comes back to the start and then, just like that, you hear a click and the door opens. That's what a formula is: different doors opening.'

Adam nodded to himself. The formula of his life was a jumble and he was finding it difficult to solve. Mrs Green's voice rang out in his head once more.

'You know, Adam, you're not bad at maths; in fact you're better than average. Your challenge is, you're not so good at showing me how you did it. You're not so good at the working out.'

'But I get the marks for the correct answer, right?'

'Yes, of course. If the answer is correct. But if it's not, you get none of the marks if you don't show your workings. And sometimes the working it out is more interesting than the end result. Do you understand?'

'What you thinking about?' asked William, looking over at Adam.

'Numbers, formulas, equations.'

'Oh yeah? Work anything out?' William smiled to himself.

After a pause, Adam shook his head and laughed.

'Oh yeah, I get it. You're funnier than you used to be. They replaced your heart, but not your funny bone,' replied Adam, a little grin pulling at his lips.

Smiling at William, Adam felt calm once again. William's presence secured him, making him feel anchored, and although Adam did still disappear into the silent land, he did so much less when William was around.

'Look, I'm glad you came anyway. I wanted to show you something. I managed to get one of the guys at the abattoir to sort it for me . . . Anyway, if you think it's stupid, you can just say so.'

'What is it?' asked William, sitting up on his stool.

Adam opened the door to the freezer room and disappeared, emerging a few minutes later with a wrapped and bloody parcel. He placed the parcel onto the chopping board and slowly unwrapped it, revealing a heart – large, bloody and no longer beating.

William gasped and recoiled. 'I'm sorry, I just thought you might be interested in seeing one,' said Adam worriedly.

'No, no, it's OK,' replied William, gathering himself. 'I . . . I just wasn't expecting it.'

Leaning over the bloodstained chopping board, both Adam and William stared at the organ in front of them.

'It's a sheep's heart. I read somewhere that it's the closest thing to a human heart, only bigger,' whispered Adam.

'It's so ugly,' observed William.

'Yeah, but there's something about it that makes it . . .'

'Powerful.'

'Yeah. Powerful like an engine in a car. So many different valves and arteries and filters. Pour blood in and it comes to life.'

The heart lay there under the glare of the gently humming lights. Without realising it, William had his hand on his chest, feeling for his heartbeat. Visions of his heart being shocked into life flooded his brain.

'This is what my old heart must have ended up like. Dead and discarded. Where do they all go, all the dead hearts?' asked William, still clutching his chest.

Wrapping up the parcel once more, Adam put it back in the freezer.

'I'm sorry, I didn't want to upset you. I just thought it might help somehow.'

William moved away from the counter and sat back on the stool.

'You know, in some strange way, it has. To see it like that. I know it for what it is now. An engine. Imperfect and prone to failing. Makes you realise some things are more important than physical things.' As Adam and William left the shop, locking the door behind them, Adam realised what the constant sound of the humming freezers reminded him of. It was the tone of a flatline – the fatal sound that a heart was no longer beating.

Adam looked over the crammed trains. He threw the spray can down onto his rucksack and smiled. He was done, finished. It had taken him months of scraped knees and elbows and a sore back, but he had never felt more alive than he was now, surrounded by darkness. Looking out, he saw the clouds breaking slowly to reveal flashes of violet and blue. Adam felt at a turning point. Then the euphoric feeling deserted him. He doubled over, hands on knees, feeling emotional and tired.

'What you doing up there?'

The familiar voice broke through the tiredness and spun Adam around. Standing at the foot of the train, with wild hair and flashing eyes, was Laila, chin jutting out and shoulders set back. Adam folded his arms across his chest.

'What are you doing here?' he asked.

'I came to see you. As you have so many secrets and don't like sharing, I thought I'd find out for myself.'

'It wasn't a secret, it was just . . . something I had to do.'

'Oh. But in secret, right? One of those things boys do, right, in secret. See a man about a dog, or come to disused rail yards and spend hours on top of trains. Did you ever think I would like to know where you disappeared after school every day?'

'Um . . .'

'Did you ever think I would worry about you? Think you were in trouble?'

'I was going to tell you . . . I wanted to. I just . . .'

'Just forgot, or decided not to, or did your stupid boy thing of keeping it to yourself.'

'You stopped talking to me. Started avoiding me, and took up with Faze. I didn't know what to do. You chose him. It's up to you.'

Laila's eyes flashed, a thunderous look clouded her face, and although the clouds were breaking overhead, it was her expression that forecast a storm.

'Don't you understand ANYTHING?! You don't tell me anything that's going on in your life. I know your Dadda has died, but that's it. The rest is a big black hole. How am I supposed to be there for you if I don't know what's wrong? If I don't know where you go. What you're thinking. How? Faze . . . was around and talked to me. He was standing up for you. Don't you get it? He told me about some of the things that had . . . happened to you when you were growing up. He said he liked you and he missed being friends with you, but his life was different now. He wished it could be like it was, but he knows you're different. He stays away from you, because he doesn't want to bring you down. Can't you see?'

Adam's mind was spinning. 'I just saw you two together and . . . then other things happened. I don't know about anything. I feel closer to violence than happiness sometimes. And I feel so far from you.'

Laila shook her head. 'Don't you see, Adam? I'm on your side. We all are.'

Adam looked down at Laila. The distance between them was only a short drop, but it felt like a chasm. Adam stared up at the large estate towering above them. Laila had now sat down and was looking up at him.

'Do you know anybody who lives in that block?' he asked.

She nodded. 'Yeah, a cousin of mine lives up there, near the top. Saira.'

Grinning, Adam hooked on his rucksack and climbed down from the train.

'Perfect. Let's go,' he said, grabbing Laila's arm and pulling her along.

'Where?' she replied, flustered.

'I want to show you what I've been doing here these last few months,' Adam replied, looking over his shoulder and smiling as they entered the block of flats.

'Why can't you show me from down here?' asked Laila, pulling her hand out of Adam's grasp.

'Trust me, you'll see why.' Pressing the lift button, Adam waited. Nothing happened, Adam pressed again. Still nothing. Laila looked at him.

'You know the lifts in these blocks are always broken . . .'

Adam took a step towards the stairs.

'What floor does she live on? We need to see out, and we can't do that unless we're in one of the flats that faces out onto the rail yard. Text her . . .'

Laila texted her and waited. A few seconds later her phone buzzed and she nodded at Adam.

'She's in. It's the twenty-fourth floor. Adam, can't we just see it from down here . . . ?'

'No. You have to see it from up there. Come on.' Adam took hold of her hand again and bounded up the stairs. As the floors went by, Adam spoke to Laila. He told her everything. About his father hurting them and then leaving them and now wanting to see him. About Farah and her silence and her love. About his mum and her coldness with him. About his grandfather and his distance from them. About William and the heart and washing the body and the funeral and the loan sharks and the police station and everything. By the time he had finished, Adam was shaking, fingers trembling. It was so much easier when he didn't have to look at her. Looking into her eyes would undo him, so he paced up the stairs holding her hand tightly and telling her so many things. Things he had told no one else.

Laila followed, scarcely breathing so as not to interrupt Adam as he talked. Each step became a sentence, each landing a paragraph and each floor a new chapter. The higher they went, the slower they climbed, each step beginning to hurt, just as each sentence was harder to say. As they lifted themselves out from the depths of the street and began to see glimpses of the violet sky, Adam's voice broke a few times, but he climbed on, not daring to look back. Laila didn't object, even though her calves were burning, even though each step was agony and even though all she wanted to do was gather Adam in her arms and hold him, high above the street, away from the gutter down below.

Adam kept on talking, telling Laila everything, holding nothing back. The floors passed them by like horses on a carousel leaping up and down, but there was no music, just his voice echoing in the stairwell of the tower block. He knew she would be listening, he knew she would be upset and want to comfort him and he knew she would be hurting, having to climb up all this way, but what other way was there? He had to tell her and he had to show her.

By the twenty-third floor, they were both sucking in lungfuls of air. Taking the last few steps before the twenty-fourth floor they dragged themselves into the corridor. Adam sat down and leaned against the cold grey wall, pulling his knees in. Laila sat cross-legged in front of him. Putting her hand on his knees, she shook them gently.

'It's not your fault. Any of it. You're carrying it around with you like a rucksack full of heavy rocks. You walk like you're carrying a big weight. Your head is always bent low, looking at the ground. But it's not your fault. Lift up your head and look at me. It's. Not. Your. Fault.'

Lifting his head, Adam looked right into Laila's eyes. The storm had subsided, leaving the calm ripples of sunlight playing on water. This was the closest she'd ever been to him, and he noticed her bottom teeth were slightly uneven. They stayed like that for a time, sucking in air, letting tired limbs relax and beating hearts catch a normal rhythm. Putting her hand on Adam's chest, Laila sat up on her knees and leaned in until their foreheads were touching.

'Can you feel my heartbeat?' asked Adam.

'Yes. It has a strong rhythm,' she replied.

'William says he's all out of heart. He's got nothing else to give.'

'You're all heart, Adam. You have nothing but heart. Let yourself see it.'

Laila looked at Adam and smiled. Pulling him in close, she brushed Adam's brow with her lips.

'Now, we climbed all this way to see something, didn't we?'

Nodding, Adam stood up and grabbed her hand.

Laila knocked on number 117 and waited. A girl opened the door and smiled. Seeing Adam, she frowned.

'You all right? You're not preggers, are you?' asked Saira.

'No!' replied Laila, laughing. 'We just need to see something out of your living-room window. Are your mum and dad in?'

'Nah, they're at Auntie Nasreen's, innit. The lifts broke so they'll stay over. Did you two climb up here?'

'Yeah,' replied Laila, stealing a glance at Adam, who looked a bit sheepish.

'For real, you climbed up?! Craaazy. You'd better come in, eh.'

Saira turned to Adam.

'What can you see from up here that you can't see from down there . . . ?'

Adam approached the window, just a few feet away. As he edged closer, the familiar blood-red colour filled his vision. Putting both hands on the window-sill, he laughed, the sound filling the room. He heard Laila approach, the gasp that escaped from her throat, the shock that filled his ears. Saira was next, still confused about what was happening. Standing next to Laila she pointed down, eyes widening.

'You . . . Is that . . . you? Did you do that?'

'Yeah. It was me,' Adam replied, unable to tear his gaze away.

'We've been watching it for months. Each day I wake up and there'd be a little bit more. At the beginning we tried to guess what it would be, but nobody could. People been talking about it up and down the tower.'

Laila looked down at the image in front of her. A stretched canvas of trains on which was painted a giant heart with arteries and ventricles, but that was not all.

'It's a fist too,' said Saira. 'Can you see it? When the sun goes down and it's all shaded and shadowy, you can see a fist in the heart or it turns into a fist, I don't know. I stare at it when I come home until it gets dark.'

Laila leaned into Adam and shook her head.

'You been doing all that, all these months. It's incredible,' she said, her voice cracking with emotion.

Adam looked down at his work. The sun was closing fast now and the image was turning from a crimson heart into a shaded fist, as Saira had said. It had worked. He hadn't been sure if it would, but it had.

Turning to Laila, he shrugged. 'I don't know why I did it.'

'With you, I get the feeling there will always be times when you don't know why.'

Saira looked from Adam to Laila and shook her head. 'If you ain't preggers, you soon will be if you carry on like that.'

Laila pretended to cuff her and laughed.

'We'd better go,' said Adam reluctantly.

They said goodbye to Saira and turned to leave.

'Saira, you can't tell anyone it was Adam. Promise?'

Saira held up her hands. 'I can't promise nothing like that,' she protested.

'You have to, otherwise he'll get arrested. You know that. Promise me.'

'OK, I promise,' replied Saira, rolling her eyes.

Laila hugged her and said goodbye. Turning to Adam, she slipped her hand into his.

'Going down?' she asked.

Adam laughed. 'Going down's going to be a lot easier than coming up.'

'True, but it was worth the climb, wasn't it?'

'Yeah, it really was,' replied Adam, taking the first step.

*'Only from the heart can
you touch the sky.'*

Rumi

Adam felt them before he saw them. Two blocks of shadow emerging to stand in his way. They would expect him to plead, to ask for more time, to run, to cry. The canal path was quiet and deserted. No talk, nothing worth saying as they grabbed him and held him, lifting him off his feet. No fists, not this time. This time they had to make a statement. He knew it, sensed it, but he didn't know what the statement would be. They knew their business, these two. A few bruises sometimes, a few cuts some other times and a few broken bones all other times. But this time they had snippets of information that meant being creative in their punishment. Which meant making a symbolic statement. Now they were speaking, shouting scalding words meant to scare but which made no difference to Adam, but there was something else, something about the way they held on to his arm and hand. His left hand, his drawing hand. Now for the first time there was fear, now there was the beginning of panic, but he was too proud, his will too strong to show this, to cry out. They mouthed words, grinning, letting the idea settle in Adam's head, a little seed sprouting thorns in his mind, pricking the walls of his imagination, and then he knew. He knew what they intended, and from far, far away he admired their brutal creativity. Their need to find answers was as urgent as his. Their willingness to use whatever tools they had to hand was impressive. Adam shook his head in wonder, smiling. That stopped them for a brief moment as they took in his calm, his wonder at their imagination. But it was brief. He felt himself falling, his left hand being pulled out in front of him. The larger shadow sat on him, fixing him to the ground as the smaller shadow pinned his left hand at the wrist, a brick in his free hand. A russet-coloured brick the same colour as every house on Marrow Street. Adam flexed his fingers, his flaring hand imitating the movement of a floating jellyfish. The flickering beating of a heart. Looking Adam right in the eye, the smaller shadow brought the brick down.

'Step away before you get rushed, dun kno,' said Tank, Strides standing next to him.

Brick looked up, eyes narrowed, and turned to Block.

'Walk away, bruv. Nuttin to do with you.'

'He's one of ours, bruv, and you just hurt him. Step away from him before you get touched.' Strides took a step forward, but Tank held out a hand to halt him. Block leaned down and whispered something into Brick's ear.

'I know you, fam, but this is official business – his family owes us. Ain't no disrespect to you, bruv. We just the messengers,' said Brick.

'You broke his hand. His tagging hand, bruv. That's some deep message.'

Strides walked up to Brick and eyeballed him, inches away. Brick held his ground.

'You know our family, bruv. Orders is orders, you get me.'

Tank walked up to stand beside Strides and pointed his finger in Brick's face. Block stood nervously to one side, looking from Brick to Tank.

'I know your don and he knows me, fam. He knows my name.'

'Business is business,' replied Brick.

'Tell him, if he wants to discuss this business to come see me.'

Brick took a step back and nodded.

'All right, yeah. I'll tell him.'

Brick and Block backed away, watching Tank and Strides.

'Next time I see you, cuz, it won't be about business,' said Tank.

Brick nodded but carried on walking, with Block still looking over his shoulder at Strides.

Adam lay in a foetal position, his broken hand nestled into his chest. He had made out snippets of the exchange between Tank and Brick. Strides came over and gently helped him to stand. Tank brushed him down and looked at him.

'This not the place for you, fam. Come. Let's get that hand sorted.'

'Never know, might add some new angles to my spraying,' replied Adam.

Tank shook his head, but what Adam remembered the most was not the pain filling his head, but Strides's growling laughter echoing in the canal tunnels as they walked back into the light.

*In under a minute your heart can pump
blood to every cell in your body.*

Adam watched as his mum paced the length of the living room, arms folded across her chest, lips pursed. He looked over at William, who shrugged and shook his head. Adam looked down at his notepad, flicking through the pages at the hundreds of little drawings he had sketched. A lot of them were of Farah bent over her low table joining up the dots in her book. Some were of William with his right hand hooked over his shoulder, protecting his heart. There were many of Laila, sitting on a park bench, leaning against a wall, smiling, grinning, hands fluttering. There were a lot of Laila, Adam thought, smiling to himself. He flicked through, trying to spot sketches of his mum, and realised for the first time that every drawing of her was a silhouette, a shadowy scratched-out blur. And in each she was either ironing or cutting onions or hoovering or folding clothes. Always straightening out, cleaning up, putting away. Adam tried to remember if she had always been like this, or if she'd changed since his dad had left. In all of his drawings, he had never once drawn her face. She never stood still long enough for him to draw her at rest. She stopped pacing for a moment to look at Adam's hand, now bound in a cast.

It was only Adam's insistence that he would sort it that had stopped her going to the police. Brick and Block hadn't been around again, but he knew it was only a matter of time. Adam had made some enquiries about the money owed, with as yet no answers. But he had one more person to ask. Yasmin turned on her heel and walked out of the living room.

'What's up with her?' asked William, keeping his voice low.

'Dunno. There was a phone call earlier . . .'

'Maybe we should go out to give her some space?'

Farah looked up at them as they whispered and came to sit in William's lap. Burrowing her head into his chest, she signed, expressively yet concerned. William still couldn't sign, but was getting better at understanding her.

She's not happy because people are talking about her.

'What people, Farah?' asked Adam.

People. Just people all around.

'What are they saying?' asked William.

Horrible things about her, like they did before.

'But she doesn't usually care about that stuff. She's heard it all before. She stopped caring about all of that years ago. There must be something else.'

She's angry about the other things they've been saying.

'What other things, Farah?'

About William. She pointed.

'What have they been saying about me?' asked William.

I don't know. Just things about him and us and her and me. Horrible things.

218

'I'll be back in a while,' said Yasmin, voice sailing through the corridor and into the living room. The door slammed behind her, making Farah jump.

'I'm going to follow her,' said Adam, pulling on his trainers.

'I'll come with you,' replied William.

Me too, signed Farah.

William looked at Adam and shrugged. 'We can't leave Farah here, can we?'

'Come on, Farah, shoes on. Let's go, quick before we lose her.' Adam was already moving towards the door.

Yasmin was marching down the street, skirts swirling around her. Adam, William and Farah followed at a safe distance. Taking a left at the end of the street, she crossed over. William clutched Farah's hand as they crossed the road, following in Yasmin's footsteps.

'I know where she's going,' said Adam. 'She's going to the community centre.'

'Why there?' asked William.

'Because that's where they meet. The do-gooders who decide who's good and who isn't. They have meetings where they discuss "things". To give a verdict without a trial.'

William watched the slight form of Yasmin striding up the street and felt his heart jump. He'd never seen her truly angry, not in a loud and terrible way, but he knew her anger simmered under the surface.

Yasmin stood outside the entrance to the community centre she had been to many times before for weddings, engagements, birthdays, following deaths and for numerous other functions.

A centre that was supposed to be all things for all people in the community. Yasmin pulled the door open and strode past a confused-looking receptionist. Something in Yasmin's eyes told the woman it would be best to let her pass.

'Should we go in?' asked Adam, trying to peer through to see where his mum had gone.

William stood still, uncertain.

'Come on, let's go in,' Adam said eventually. They heard voices in the main hall and ducked left, making sure they weren't seen at the reception. Adam knew a way up to the gallery, where they could see and hear everything. Down below was a gathering of people old and young sitting on chairs. At the front was a short man talking in a loud voice. Adam knew him; it was Mr Akhtar, he lived four doors down from them. The curtain always twitched when you walked past his house. Adam wasn't really sure what he did, but he did know that he worked at knowing what everyone in the whole neighbourhood was doing. There was a little stage in the hall set up for meetings and performances, and the man strode around the stage using every inch of it. Holding court, making the most of the opportunity to be listened to. Everybody wanted to be listened to, but surely there were better ways than this. The man continued to talk about the difficulties of being a part of a community and staying close to your friends and family. Farah nudged Adam and made a yapping sign with her hands and pretended to be falling asleep. Adam smiled and nodded in agreement. Then his speech began to take another turn and Adam heard his Dadda's name being mentioned.

'As you all know, since Abdul-Aziz died, that poor family has suffered. We all know that. *But*. The goings-on in that household have to be discussed. We, as a community, have a responsibility to uphold our values and help others who have lost their way or are struggling to cope. I know we don't live in a perfect world and that we have problems with other families in our community, but there's a limit to what we can observe and not take action. I can see some of you nodding. You understand, don't you? This is an extreme case, but I think we can help. Over the last few months, I've seen police visit their house, I've seen two men who looked quite dangerous and a lot of trouble visit and loiter outside the house, but most worryingly of all, almost every single day I've seen a man – I know some of you have seen him also – visiting the Shah house. When he first started visiting, I thought maybe he was a solicitor or social worker. You see? We are modern enough to understand that these things are needed. But he came every day, and that was worrying. I am not one to interfere, so I said nothing to anyone, but then I began to see him walking the streets with the little one, Farah. Holding her hand and taking her to the shops to buy sweets. And some days I see him entering the house, but not leaving until the next morning. I was shocked, let me tell you. I began to wonder what kind of hold this man had on the family. It was such a shock to me, I admit, when I saw the two of them walking towards the park; I called the police because I was so concerned. I followed this up by calling up the police and asking who he was, and they explained that he was "a friend of the family". And now I have found out the truth. You all know that Abdul-Aziz Shah decided to leave his heart to be donated. That was shocking enough for most of us to hear. But this man I've seen wandering around, he was the one to receive it.'

The hush that had settled on the assembled crowd was broken by a few gasps and muttered prayers.

'I was in shock too. But what could I do? I wanted to be discreet, but felt this could only be solved as a community. The mother, Yasmin Shah, we know has a troubled past. Being separated from your husband can't be easy, and then trying to raise two children . . . We can all understand how it is for a woman alone. But still, to take a man into your house and let him roam the streets free with your child . . . It is too much. She needs our help.'

Adam was so angry he wanted to hurl a chair over the banister right at Mr Akhtar so that it would land square on his head and shut him up. Even Farah looked agitated and annoyed that this man could say such things. Only William looked calm and sat leaning against some stacked chairs, shaking his head. He held up a hand to placate Adam.

'He doesn't know what he's talking about,' he said quietly.

Now a seated figure had stood up and was walking towards the stage. Adam stood up too. It was Yasmin.

William was staring right at Yasmin and saw the expression on her face.

'She's going to kill him,' he said.

'Let's hope so,' said Adam, scowling.

Yasmin had wrapped a scarf around her face to keep from being recognised and hung back at the edge of the room, keeping to the shadows. Stepping towards Mr Akhtar, Yasmin let the scarf drop. There was another gasp, but this time it was uncomfortable and there was a lot more shuffling. Yasmin looked out over the crowd, defiant, eyes resting on each face, letting them know she had taken note of who was there. Turning to Mr Akhtar, she laughed, the sound echoing around the hall, bouncing off the walls and filling all the awkward spaces in between.

'Is this how it's done then?' she asked. 'A nice cosy discussion about all the problems in the community. A nice informal chat with tea and samosas and some homemade chutney. Make you feel better, does it, discussing our "problems"? Make you feel as if you're part of the solution, does it? Is this supposed to be community work? Where were you when I needed you? Where were you when my family needed you? You all knew about my husband. You all knew what he was doing, what he was into. You all knew that he hit me, beat me, he . . . hurt me, hurt Adam, Farah . . . she was hurt by him . . . How could you not see? Did you call the police then? When you saw me walk to the shops with my bruised face. Did you call a meeting then? But you'd rather smear this man. This innocent man, whose name is William, who walked into our lives. Who has been nothing but good to us. He has said little, hasn't judged us and we haven't judged him. We accepted him and he us. He appeared and he stayed. Which one of you was willing to do that for us? He is part of our family, both physically and spiritually – do you understand?'

Adam held the banisters with such an iron grip that they started to wobble. He was scared of what he might do if he let go. He felt a hand on his arm and looked to see Farah smiling up at him, defusing his rage. He sat back and looked over at William. In the half-light of the gallery, Adam could see two tears, one from each eye, track their way down William's face.

Two silent tears, Two tears silent,
Too silent tears.

Turning back to his mum, Adam understood what it had cost her to come here. Why she had been muttering to herself. She had such spirit – too much, Dadda had always said – but what if he had said instead that she had the right amount of spirit. To be somebody. To look after the family. Despite everything. But he never had. It had always been too much spirit.

Mr Akhtar stood with his mouth open, hands hanging slack at his sides. He had visibly flinched when Yasmin had stepped onto the stage. His mouth was making strange shapes as he tried to say something, anything, to appease the angry, upright figure in front of him.

'Where are your words now? Here I am – help me. Help me to understand. Help me and my family to be *in* the community rather than the talk of the community. Help me to move out from the dark shadow of my husband. Help us understand my father's actions. Help us look up to the sky, look forward. Because that's why you're here, right? To help.'

Mr Akhtar began to wring his hands, and some people began to mutter among themselves. The show was over, and Yasmin looked once more over the faces in the crowd.

'I grew up with your daughters and sons. I've eaten at your houses, attended your weddings. You've come here today because you're ashamed of me. Let me tell you something: I'm ashamed of you.'

Stepping off the stage, Yasmin wrapped the scarf around her head, threw it over her shoulder and, without looking back, stormed out of the hall.

Adam stared out over the shocked crowd. Farah tugged at his T-shirt and rubbed her eyes. Picking her up and holding her close, he led the three of them out of the hall and they followed Yasmin home.

Farah came down the stairs and sat on the bottom step. Setting her big book aside, she looked at her mother. Signing with deliberate care, Farah pointed at her. *I'm worried about you. You look sad and quiet.* Coming to sit next to her on the bottom step, Yasmin smiled.

'You don't have to worry. I'm OK. I'm always OK.'

Farah squinted and looked at her, making her laugh, the sound filling the air.

'Now, are you going to put away your book for a little while and help me put fresh sheets on the beds?'

Farah nodded and smiled. *I like sleeping in fresh sheets. It feels like everything is brand new.*

Yasmin put her arm around Farah. 'You're right, I do too. Let's go and make everything brand new again, at least for a while.'

The Greeks believed the heart was the seat of the spirit, the Chinese associated it with happiness and the Egyptians thought the emotions and intellect arose from the heart.

Farah woke with a start. There was a dull thrum from the machine next to her, a tube inserted into her arm. Next to her, curled up awkwardly in a low chair, was Adam, his black hoodie wrapped around him. Farah couldn't see his face, just a shock of black hair. In the dimmed greenish light of the ward, it looked like a piece of night sat crumpled in the corner. Her head hurt. She remembered now. Her head hurt so much that she could no longer see. She remembered how each thought sent flashing pains zigzagging into her brain. She remembered how she could no longer make out shapes, no longer see her mum, William or Adam. The last thing she remembered was how she could no longer see the dot-to-dots in her book. They had been dancing around on the page, off the page, in front of her eyes. She had tried to swat them away. Had tried to catch a few of them and put them back on the page. William had been the first to notice. Always watching, always listening. Like her. He had been first to see that she wasn't being herself. They had all come into the room then, and Farah had tried to explain.

Had pointed to the book, and the jumping numbers, but the pain in her head had exploded, and after that she remembered nothing more. The pain was still there, but duller, further away. A memory flashed in her head, making her wince. Was it her memory? She remembered it clearly. Farah fought against sleep but it came flooding back and took her away, to when she was five years old and she remembered falling . . .

I live in the silent land the silent land the silent land where everything is drawn by my hand and where everything is old and new and quiet so quiet and connected to everything else dot to dot to dot to point to point to point to you to me to we to I and them and us them and us and us and them a world in white a world in dots and numbers a new world waiting waiting half finished waiting to be finished and me the drawer the scribbler the dot to dotter the point to pointer the maker line maker the incredible the fantastic the line defying pencil pushing pencil twirling joiner the pencil breaker the lead blotcher the picture completer the greatest of all lines is mine HB fine so fine until the end of time until the end of time.

A bigger heart is not a better heart.

The doctors explained that Farah had an inflammation in her brain due to a blood clot, probably caused by the fall she had suffered and most likely the cause of her reluctance to speak, as it had affected her brain function and her ability to make speech connections. They had said that they would wait to see how Farah would respond to treatment and whether the inflammation would reduce. Adam looked over at Yasmin, a little crinkly mess in the low chair, scarf wrapped around her head and covering part of her face. A cowl to shut out the world. She had barely left the hospital, despite William's insistence that she go home and rest. Yasmin had smiled kindly and said that 'a mother can't go home, William'. Adam and William had come and gone, bringing fresh clothes for Yasmin and staying for a while before leaving. For William, hospitals were places of death, but he also knew them to be places where life bloomed or was reignited. Feeling a gentle hand on his shoulder, he turned to see Adam smiling down at him.

'You look terrible,' said Adam.

'Thanks,' replied William, returning the smile.

Adam went over to his mum and knelt down at her feet so she could talk to him quietly. *Give him a hug*, thought William, *hold his hand, push the hair away from his face, anything! Just show him you care! I know you care, just show him!* William shook his head to clear it. Yasmin whispered to Adam, who nodded.

'Mum said we need to go home so you can rest, William. Seriously. You don't look great and you know that you need to take care.'

'I'll feel bad if I leave.'

'Just for a little while. We'll come back with some food and clothes later tonight. Come on,' urged Adam.

Yasmin made a shooing gesture to the pair of them.

'OK, let's go home, but we'll come back in a while,' said William, reluctantly standing up. He followed Adam out of the ward and down the corridor into the street, Adam keeping in step with him and trying not to rush him by walking ahead. He helped William onto the bus and into a front seat closest to the door.

These last few weeks, William had been a different person. A person who laughed, cracked jokes, helped out around the house. He was finally taking part in life and, despite the strange circumstances, he was enjoying it. But Farah's illness had hit him hard, a heavyweight punch just under the heart, shaking him to the core. The light in his eyes had diminished a little and his belief in the life he had adopted had dimmed.

On the walk home from the bus stop, William stumbled. Grabbing his arm, Adam propped William against his shoulder.

'It's OK, William, we're almost there.'

'No – this doesn't feel right. Take me back to the hospital. I want to be with Farah. Please.'

Adam looked into William's ashen face and held up his hands.

'OK, William, we'll go to the hospital. Just hold tight. I'll get us a cab.'

The cab driver helped Adam half carry, half drag William through the emergency-room doors. Slumping him down, he looked at Adam and puffed out his cheeks.

'No fare. Hope he'll be OK,' he said, and patting William on the shoulder he left.

'Take me to Farah,' whispered William, tugging feebly at Adam's sleeve.

'We're taking you to a doctor first. We'll see Farah later, I promise,' replied Adam, trying to spot a nurse.

William clutched at his shirt and groaned, sliding down his chair and sagging to the floor. A doctor came striding over and knelt down beside him. Barking a few sort, sharp instructions to the nurses, he called for a gurney.

'I'm with him. Doctor, he's with me.' Adam was panicking. 'Will he be OK? What's the matter with him?'

'He looks like he's having a heart attack.'

'No, that's not possible.'

'What do you mean?'

'He has a good heart in there – a transplant. A strong heart. It can't have gone bad. It can't.'

The doctor narrowed his eyes and patted Adam's shoulder. 'Look, don't worry; we'll look after him. He's in the right place.'

'You don't understand. He's got a new heart, a good heart. It was my Dadda's.'

'I can see he's had a transplant. Please take a seat. We'll take it from here and we'll keep you informed. Please, take a seat.'

'No. I'm staying with him. There's no one else. Do you understand?'

'OK, sure,' replied the doctor, nodding at the nurses to roll William away.

Putting a hand on William's chest and feeling the rough texture of the scarred skin, Adam willed himself to smile.

'It's all right, William, just a precaution. You know how they like saying that in hospitals. You've had a bit of shock and it just caught you unawares.'

'Farah – I need to see her . . .'

'Yeah, we're going to see her. Just hold on.'

In less than five minutes, William was in a ward and plugged in to the hospital's mainframe. The combination of drip, monitor and oxygen meant he was connected to life. Sinking down in a low chair beside the bed, Adam sighed, muttering to himself, 'I hate hospitals.'

I'm sure this has happened to others and others but
it has happened to me and him and them and us
and so and so the day the door opened I saw and
she saw that he was gonna stay and stay and I was
not OK with that not OK not not OK and now now
that he's going to go I'm not OK with that not OK
not OK and I remember seeing her in the hospital
the day after and she was screaming screaming no
longer able lungs on fire and it wasn't talking but
it was screaming and alive and screaming and her
foot in my hand was tiny and I was only tiny small
tiny but still she gripped my finger and coughed
and screamed and he wasn't there was elsewhere
elsewhere angry man was elsewhere all fists and fits
of angry fists beating down beat down into soft
flesh her flesh my flesh flesh of our flesh and still
we lived on Marrow long street Marrow shoulder
to shoulder toe to toe to toe watching others news

reporting watching others news and life went on and on and he was angry and the other he was sad angry and sad and we watching growing gaining taller shorter drawing on the lead broken lead drawing with broken stubs scraping on walls drawing on my head inside my head and onto cave walls scenes from my head and her head of hurt and punch after punch and hurt and slap after slap and hurt and kick after kick and so much for forever and forever and till death do us do us good and proper until the fat lady sings but she prays and prays and prays and pushes prayer into the air pushes a ball around a chain per second per tick per tick tock one beat on the beat one beat on the beat and he sits in a chair that is his not his and sinks and sinks and sinks throwing anchor after anchor after anchor overboard man overboard into the sink drowning drowning and there's no saving for after no afters apart from the afters we all feel him me and them and us the sinking down into the sink without a plughole don't plug the hole let all of it drain into the vortex of blood and water and blood and water and she sits and watches me and tips her head head tipping into the future and I do the head shake into the past don't watch me don't watch this this isn't one to watch one for the future a future star watch yourself watch your self casting shadows onto the wall and ask said shadow your questions don't ask me I'm only flesh and blood and mix and blood ask

240

the shadow all questions about the future shadows stick shadows follow shadows long and tall shadows grow and bend shadows lie in wait shadows never die shadows never die.

It had been seven months since William had been given a new heart. Dr Desai couldn't explain whether his body had rejected the heart or the heart had rejected his body, but it was plain that rejection was the catchword. William's body felt as if it had been at war. Abdul-Aziz Shah's heart had revolted. Claret waves had crashed against a cliff-face, attacking the atria and surging through the ventricles. William was left washed up on the shore, bleached and raw.

William watched as Mrs Shah, Daddima, sat in a chair a few paces from his bed. She was wearing a coal-black woollen overcoat and a sombre navy-blue tunic top with billowy trousers, and the usual white scarf, one end of which was flung over her left shoulder. She looked ashen and vulnerable. She felt William's eyes upon her and began to speak. William didn't speak Urdu, but he understood. It was a lament. Mrs Shah spoke about her life, her choices, her desires. She shook her head and pursed her lips when she spoke of Yasmin, but her eyes were defiant. She cried when she spoke of Farah and stopped to wipe her eyes with the end of her scarf. When she spoke of Mr Shah, the tone changed, becoming inaudible, breathless as she lowered her eyes and spoke to the floor. William listened to the rippling cadence of Mrs Shah's voice in the half-light of the ward and slept.

When he opened his eyes once more, Yasmin was standing over him, peering at his face. Mrs Shah still sat her vigil in the chair. Her lips were moving rapidly and her face was creased in concentration. Adam, gripping his notepad, was perched on the end of his bed. All three were watching William, who raised his eyebrows in greeting.

'We thought that was it for you, William,' said Yasmin.

'Yes. Almost. How is she? Where is she?' asked William.

A tired smile crept onto Yasmin's face as she looked towards the ward entrance. Farah was being wheeled in by a nurse, large book in hand, her head tightly bandaged and showing spots of blood. Seeing William, Farah's face illuminated and for a moment Ward 38 was filled with something other than the weight of imminent death.

'We have to take her back very soon,' said the nurse.

Gently as he could, Adam lifted Farah out of her wheelchair and placed her near William. Setting her book and pen down, Farah held William's left hand and unbuckled his watch. Holding the watch to her right ear, she nestled into William's chest, legs tucked in, making herself as small as possible. As he had done before, William enveloped her with his arms as she listened to the trickle of his heart-beat.

After a while, William looked to see Yasmin shifting her weight from foot to foot.

'Why did he do it? Why did he give away his heart?' he asked.

Yasmin looked at William and sat down on the end of the bed. Farah had disentangled herself and opened her book. Both William and Yasmin stopped to watch her little hand's jerky progress across the page.

Yasmin looked away.

'I never told you, but it was my mum who gave the consent for the heart donation. Dad made her swear an oath so that she'd go through with it. It almost broke her. My dad had regrets, William. It frustrated him. I always felt that physically he was here with us but mentally he was away, walking with his disappointments. He wasn't the best father or husband, but he always wanted to do the right thing. He had a good heart and that counts for something, doesn't it?'

William looked up at that, but Yasmin was looking at something else, somewhere else.

'Yes, that counts,' he replied, watching her. She didn't see him smile.

Adam stood watching William, halfway between the bed and the door. One foot in this world and one in the next – William knew how that was. Using all his strength, William propped himself up and signalled for Adam to come closer. Adam shuffled towards the bed and stood over William. Taller now and wiser but more hurt, left hand nestled into his body. Black and bruised eyes regarded him. William had hoped it would be different for this boy, that it could be better. He had hoped to stick around and see to it.

'You're off then,' said Adam quietly.

'I reckon so.'

'To the silent land . . . ?'

'Nah. I'm done being silent.'

'You're not going to start telling your awful jokes there, are you?'

'It might be a start,' replied William, smiling. 'You gonna be all right?'

'Yeah. Getting used to all this coming and going.'

'You're the best lad,' whispered William.

'I'm not the best anything.'

William shook his head. 'It's not your fault.'

'I left the door open,' replied Adam, glancing at Farah. 'And look what happened.'

'You remember the times you told me about Icarus?'

'Yeah, I do. He fell too.' Adam's voice trembled.

'But in that moment when he was closest to the sun, that moment when he was hovering in the sky, he lived more in that one moment than many people do in a lifetime. Just like I've lived more in these last few months than I did in my whole life before I met you.'

Adam sank down to his knees and clasped William's hand. Leaning in close, William whispered into Adam's ear. Just one word. One last word. And the heart that was his/wasn't his, the heart that had lived two lives and that had started its steady beat so many years ago, slowed, and the heart that was a fist opened and closed and was finally allowed to rest.

Closing his eyes, William was awed to see the ward was now the brilliant white of a blank page. Faintly to begin with, and then with more definition, he saw an image scratchily emerging.

Farah, bent over her book, her small fist gripping that green pen and moving it forward, always forward. She would live. He could see that now. And where she lived, others would too. He saw Yasmin next, tightly wrapped in her layers of clothing. Standing upright, despite everything, she would see it through. She would always be there to straighten things out. Adam, all sharp angles and slashes, began to emerge next. The shadows still stuck to him, but less so now. They were muted and he saw wings unfurl from his shoulder-blades. And William knew then that Adam would fly, and if he fell he would just draw himself another pair and fly higher.

Blinking, William saw that it was his own hand jotting numbers onto the page. He saw Farah's hand following in his wake. They were all just points on a page. Daddima, Yasmin, Farah, Adam, the bed, the ward, Abdul-Aziz. Different points waiting to be connected. William watched as the picture began to take shape.

Yasmin's sense of order was restored as she stood in the middle of her bedroom. All the washing had been done, all the clothes had been ironed. Everything had been cleaned and squared away, making her feel she was still in control. This space at least she could shape. Here she could have perfection, and no matter what was going on outside, no matter how fierce the storm, it couldn't destroy the sense of calm she felt in this place. Hearing a sound behind her, she turned to see Adam watching her. His face was hidden in the shadows as he stood at the threshold of her white room.

'You straightening things out again?' he asked.

'I was just sorting a few things out. Making sure everything was where it should be.'

'But it's not, Mum. You can see that, right?'

As Adam entered the room, Yasmin caught herself grimacing. And for the first time realised that he saw it too. Had seen it many times before and had stayed quiet. But she could see the anguish in his eyes now.

'You see him, don't you, when you look at me? Each month, each year, every birthday, every day I remind you of him.' Adam looked down at his hands, spreading his fingers and holding them out in front of him as if in supplication of prayer. 'And these hands, they are the same as his. You see me and my hands, and you see them hitting you, hurting you.'

'No, Adam, it's not like that . . .'

'I am his son. But I'm not him.'

'I know you're not. You're nothing like him.'

'But in your eyes, I have become him. I can see it. And it reminds you.'

Yasmin turned to a chest of drawers and began to take out a set of towels. And with care, began to fold them again.

'Mum, what are you doing?'

'Just folding these. I need to make some room in here . . .'

'Just stop for a minute.'

'I can still talk and do this at the same time . . .'

'Yeah, but I don't want you to.'

'Look, keep talking, I'm listening—'

'No. No, you're not, you're folding. You're fixing up, straightening out, ironing out the creases . . .'

'I'm just trying to get things sorted.'

'Things can't be sorted in that way!' he shouted. Adam yanked the duvet off the bed and threw it to the ground. Grabbing a fistful of the bed-sheet, he yanked it off the mattress. He grabbed towel after towel from the drawers, flinging them to the floor. He kicked over the wash basket full of ironed clothes and threw the pillows from the bed. Breathing heavily now, he looked at the mess he had created.

At the chaos. Yasmin stood in the middle of the room, a small leafless tree still standing after a brutal storm.

Finally she spoke.

'It's a mess, Adam. I thought William could help us, but now he's gone too. It's all a mess,' Yasmin whispered.

Adam sat down and leaned against a wall, head tilted back.

'You can't iron out all the creases, Mum. You can't create a perfectly ordered world in here and ignore the world out there. You just can't.'

'You look more like him each day. You're a constant reminder of him and his need to inflict pain. But then I see you drawing with those hands, the same as his, and I know you're not him. You don't inflict pain on anyone, you create such beauty . . .'

'So see that when you look at me! See that when you see my hands and fingers! Not fists, not fury. See what I can create, not what he destroyed! Please, Mum?' Adam was pleading now.

'I try, Adam . . . It's this house, this place, your Dadda dying, William . . .' Yasmin's voice broke, tears welling up in her trembling eyes as she did her best to palm them away.

'Mum, this is our life. Imperfect, crumpled, creased and we can't just fold it and put it away.'

Yasmin came over to Adam and sat down. Putting her arm around him, she pulled him in close. Adam felt her wet cheek touch his.

'I don't want to see him when I look at you. I only want to see you and the man you will become. Only you.'

Resting his head on Yasmin's shoulder, Adam closed his

eyes. 'What a mess we're in.'

'Lucky I'm around then, isn't it?' replied Yasmin, and smiled properly for the first time in a very long time.

Laila watched Adam pacing up and down, waiting for a break in his stride so that she could reach out to him. He had barely said a word, in a way that she was getting used to. The sun was high as Adam paced, and she saw him as a silhouette driven back and forth like a shade. And that's what he was, a piece of shadow that refused to come into the light.

'What will you do?'

He stopped pacing and turned to face her. As if he'd forgotten that she had been sitting there.

'Huh?'

'What will you do? About your dad?'

'I don't know.'

Coming to sit beside her, he sat back and looked at the sky.

'I have to go see the guy who holds the debt.'

Laila stood up, blocking out the sun, her wild hair a jagged silhouette. 'Are you crazy? After what they did to your hand?'

'It's the only way I can see to get them off our backs. They said that next time they'll trash the house and hurt Mum.

I didn't believe them before, but I do now.' Adam held up his cast.

Laila's face revealed the horror she felt. 'But they'll hurt him. Hurt him bad.'

'Better than them hurting us,' Adam replied, unwavering.

It was an impossible choice, thought Laila.

'When will you go see him?'

'Now. I'm going now.'

'I'm coming with you,' she replied.

'No way!'

'They might hurt you again . . .'

'They might hurt you too. I'm not having that.'

'They're less likely to do anything if I'm there.'

'They don't care about anything like that. It means nothing.'

'I'm coming.'

'Look, just wait here . . .'

'I'm coming!'

They were both standing now and shouting.

'I'm not good at asking for help.'

'I know. But sometimes you need it. Me too.'

'Thank you. I mean it. Thank you for doing this. All of this.'

Laila nodded and together they began to walk in the direction of the square.

Adam knew where to find them. Everybody knew. His mates at school, teachers, parents, little kids, the police. Sometimes the police might arrest a couple of them, but the way it worked was: you don't bother us and we won't bother you. And on the streets and in the estates, you accepted that and you carried on. The streets had an economy, a loan system, a currency, foot soldiers, its own army. That's the way it was. You kept your mouth shut and followed the rules.

He snuck a glance at Laila walking beside him. He knew she was worried about him. He felt the pressure of living up to the expectation in her eyes. He felt the same pressure from his mum and Farah. And now he would feel it from his dad, only in a different way. It would be the disappointment of betrayal.

Brick and Block flanked the current leader of the streets, a man known as Khan. Brick had a strange look on his face as he took in Adam and his cast and the storm-eyed Laila standing at his side.

Khan sat on a low wall, smoking. He took a pull on his cigarette with deliberate care. Block bent down and whispered a few words in his ear. Taking another long pull, Khan looked up, glancing at Adam's damaged left hand.

'I see you had an accident,' said Khan.

Before Adam could answer, Laila stepped in front of him.

'If holding someone down and breaking most of the bones in their hand with a brick could be called an accident.'

Adam turned to her, but she shoved him out of the way.

'If you can call Prick and Cock here an accident of birth, we might be close to what an accident looks like . . .'

For a moment nobody spoke. Then Khan, stubbing out his cigarette, broke the silence with a sharp snort.

'Prick and Cock! That's hilarious,' he said, pointing at each one in turn. Brick and Block said nothing but they wore grim expressions.

'Now that you've insulted my boys, what can I do for you?'

Adam looked at Laila, imploring her to stay quiet.

'I want our debt settled,' he said.

'That's easy. Give me the cash and then it's done.'

'The debt's not on us. It's on someone else,' replied Adam.

'That's what they all say . . .' Khan lit another cigarette.

'It's not on us. If I can prove it, will we be square?'

'The debt's on the guy who took the bets and didn't pay. The address is yours. It's a large sum. We'll be square when I get my money.'

'The debt's not on us. We've been caught up in it. The name you were given was my grandfather's. He's dead, but it wasn't him who borrowed the money.'

'No? Who was it then?'

Glancing at Laila, Adam hesitated. Eyes gentle now, she nodded encouragement.

'My dad. He's the one who borrowed the money and gave you a fake address. He doesn't live with us. Hasn't for over three years. He's the one that kept borrowing, not us. He's nothing to do with us.'

Blowing smoke through his nose, Khan laughed.

'You've come here, to see me, to give your dad up! Are you for real, bruv?'

'The debt's not on us.'

'He's your dad,' said Khan.

'We have nothing to do with him,' countered Adam.

'You know what we'll do to him?'

'Yeah. I know.'

'Do you know where he is?'

Adam faltered. Could he give up his own dad? Knowing what they'd do to him if he couldn't pay? *Knowing* that his dad wouldn't be able to pay.

'Yes.'

Adam could see Khan weighing up the options as he stubbed out yet another cigarette.

'OK. Write down where we can find him and we'll look into it. Until we find him, the debt's still on you.'

Adam nodded and wrote down the address.

'How does it feel to grass your old man up, kid?' asked Khan.

'It feels like nothing. Absolutely nothing,' replied Adam, and turning to take Laila's hand they walked from the square and out into the space beyond.

On Marrow, long street Marrow, the shadows stretched as the sun pulsed in the cobalt sky. Farah sat on the top step, her big book resting open on her lap. Her bandage had been removed and she was finally sprouting fine tufts of hair on the top of her scalp. The doctors felt that maybe one day, with speech therapy and if she wanted, she would be able to speak. When Adam had told Farah this, she had shrugged and signed what William had said – that there wasn't always a lot worth saying. Adam nodded and smiled at the thought. It was a very William thing to say. Adam leaned against the russet brickwork, looking up at the sun, head tilted back. Laila sat on the bottom step, legs pulled up, looking at her hands. Seeing the silhouettes that flickered on the pavement, she shaped her hands into butterfly wings that played on the light grey stone. On the threshold, just behind Farah, stood Yasmin, looking out over the disorderly maze of streets. Adam smiled at her, ink-black eyes dancing. She no longer saw *him*. Now she only saw her son. She thought of William then, a memory that triggered a question.

'At the end, when William was talking to you, he whispered something in your ear . . . ?'

'Yeah. He kept it brief, as usual.'

Farah looked up at him then, and Laila broke the butterfly wings and looked up too. The sun dipped and dappled shadows fell on long street Marrow.

'What was it? What did he say?' asked Yasmin.

Adam looked up, right into the heart of the sun. Closing his eyes, Adam traced in his mind the top of the hill where Icarus stood, wings unfurled, body coiled and ready.

'Jump,' Adam replied. 'Just, jump.'

The Little Boy Found

The little boy lost in the lonely fen,
Led by the wand'ring light,
Began to cry, but God ever nigh,
Appeared like his father in white.

He kissed the child & by the hand led
And to his mother brought,
Who in sorrow pale, thro' the lonely dale,
Her little boy weeping sought.

William Blake

Irfan Master

Irfan Master's first novel, *A Beautiful Lie*, was shortlisted for the Waterstones Children's Book Prize 2011 and nominated for the Branford Boase Award 2012, as well as slew of regional awards including the North East Book Award, the We Read Award, the Essex Book Award, the Redbridge Book Award and the Amazing Book Award, all in 2012. It also featured on the 2013 USBBY Outstanding International Book Honor List. Irfan has been a librarian and was project manager of Reading the Game at the National Literacy Trust before becoming a full-time writer. Visit Irfan online at irfanmaster.com and follow @Irfan_Master on Twitter

HOT
KEY
BOOKS

Thank you for choosing a Hot Key book.

If you want to know more about our authors
and what we publish, you can find us online.

You can start at our website

www.hotkeybooks.com

And you can also find us on:

We hope to see you soon!